OPTIC NERVE

MARIA GAINZA

CATAPULT

NEW YORK

OPTIC NERVE

TRANSLATED FROM THE SPANISH BY

THOMAS BUNSTEAD

This is a work of fiction. All of the characters, organizations, and events portrayed in this novel are either products of the author's imagination or are used fictitiously.

First published in the United States in 2019 by Catapult (catapult.co)
in agreement with Casanovas & Lynch Literary Agency

Work published within the framework of "Sur" Translation Support Program of the Ministry of Foreign Affairs and Worship of the Argentine Republic.

Obra editada en el marco del Programa "Sur" de Apoyo a las Traducciones del Ministerio de Relaciones Exteriores y Culto de la República Argentina.

ISBN: 978-1-948226-16-5

Jacket design by Nicole Caputo
Book design by Wah-Ming Chang

Catapult titles are distributed to the trade by
Publishers Group West
Phone: 866-400-5351

Library of Congress Control Number: 2018956396

Printed in the United States of America
1 3 5 7 9 10 8 6 4 2

For Azucena

The visual aspect of life has always been of greater significance for me than the content.

JOSEPH BRODSKY

Just going to take a look at the painting, said Liliana Maresca after her shot of morphine.

LUCRECIA ROJAS

OPTIC NERVE

DREUX'S DEER

I first encountered Dreux on an afternoon in autumn; the deer, precisely five years later. In Dreux's case, I left the house one day under blue skies only to be caught in a sudden downpour. The narrow, winding streets of Belgrano were soon in full spate. Women clustered together on the sidewalks trying to establish the best places to cross; an old lady assailed the side of a bus with her umbrella when the driver refused to open the doors; and before long the shop owners, watching the deluge through their window displays, brought out the metal barriers they had armed themselves with after the previous flood. I was due to take some foreign tourists around a private art collection. That was my job at the time, not the worst job in the world, but that day, while I sheltered under the awning of a bar to wait for my clients, a car came past hugging the curb and drenched me and my pristine yellow dress. Three more plowed through the same puddle in quick succession, the rain stopped—as suddenly as it had begun—and of course who should pull up seconds later but my tourists? They were a middle-aged couple from the U.S. She was dressed all in white and he all in black; stepping out of the taxi they looked immaculate, improbably dry, as though they and their clothes had come directly from the dry cleaner.

We made our way to a house that had formerly been a small hotel with extensive gardens and was now boxed in between one neo-rationalist monstrosity and a lurid California-style duplex. A porter let us in and then led the way through to the living room, gliding eel-like ahead of us between the furniture. A quarter of an hour later a hidden door slid open and the owner of the collection appeared. She looked at me; I looked at her: a game of chicken she won hands down. She was dressed in gray, and her mouth had the lines of a woman bitter at finding herself the wrong side of forty. Her nose was more bladelike than aquiline, and on her cashmere sweater she wore a golden brooch of a small creature that, because of the distance she kept throughout our visit, I never managed to identify.

She looked me over with the same incredulity she had

voiced on the phone the previous night. She couldn't understand why I wanted to come when she could very well show any visitors the paintings herself. In my firm I was director, secretary, intern, and guide all rolled into one—that was how I kept things afloat, as I had tried to explain, though not in so many words. "Quite the go-getter," she had said. "Very well, see you tomorrow." And see me she did, dripping grimy water onto the gleaming parquet. She sent for some dry footwear. A few minutes later a pair of fluffy white slippers appeared, and as I stepped into them my clients' loss of respect for me was complete. My only chance: to show them how good my eye was, deliver a particularly insightful commentary, and once I got going I felt I was doing okay, more or less, until I was confronted with a dapple-gray horse, galloping straight at me under pewter skies. I glanced over at our hostess—for less than a second, but long enough:

"Alfred de Dreux." She smirked, mounting a cigarette in an ivory holder with her long, elegant fingers, almost preening. "Nineteenth century. Didn't they cover him in college?"

"Of course. A magnificent piece."

Two lies for the price of one: I had never heard of Dreux, and the piece struck me as little more than decorative. The work of someone technically gifted, but nothing more.

My clients looked back at me with identikit American smiles. Their expressions, in combination with their monochrome outfits, brought to mind the fake smiles in Jorge de la Vega's *Puzzle*.

As I say, I saw Dreux's deer for the first time five years later, on another stormy April afternoon, this time in the National Museum of Decorative Arts. I was on my own, as I always try to be when seeing something for the first time, and prepared for a washout in my chic wellington boots—ankle-cut wellington boots. Maybe it had something to do with my footwear, but this time it was fireworks, what A. S. Byatt called "the kick galvanic." It reminded me that all of art rests in the gap between that which is aesthetically pleasing and that which truly captivates you. And that the tiniest thing can make the difference. I had only to set eyes on the painting and a sensation came over me: you might describe it as butterflies, but in fact for me it's less poetic. It happens every time I feel strongly drawn to a painting. One explanation is of dopamines being released in the brain, and the consequent bump in blood pressure throughout the body, though Stendhal put it rather differently: "As I emerged from the porch of Santa Croce, I was seized with a fierce palpitation of the heart; the wellspring of life was dried up within me, and I walked in constant fear of falling to the ground." A couple of centuries later, the nurses in the emergency department at Santa Maria Nuova Hospital, shocked by the number of tourists swooning before Michelangelo's sculptures, dubbed it Stendhal syndrome.

On this second afternoon, in an attempt to keep my cool, I went out into the winter gardens. I tottered on the roof of a boat, reeling, my eyes spinning like compasses with the magnets removed. After some air I went back inside, feeling psychologically prepared this time, and it was a relief to find Dreux's deer still there. The painting hung in what had once been the Errázuriz family dining room, a baroque imitation of one of the salons at Versailles. The space was large, but not disproportionately so, and it might have been pleasantly warm if the autumn sunlight had been allowed to stream in through the garden windows, but the security guards, seeming to think an electric heater no bigger than a brick was sufficient, kept the blinds down. You could just about see your own breath.

There were in fact two paintings by Dreux in the room, both hunt scenes, both painted around the middle of the nineteenth century, but only one of them drew my eye. A doubtless reductive description would go something like this: it is a very tall piece, and in its lower portion a pack of hounds encircles a deer, while the upper panels, which look very much like they have been added as an afterthought to fit the painting to the room's high ceilings, are filled with ranked, squally clouds, a portion of blue sky, and a generic-looking tree. Fairly conventional, no point denying it, but it grabbed me nonetheless. More than that: it unsettled me.

Alfred de Dreux was seven years old when, on a walk around Siena one day with his godfather, he met the great Théodore Géricault, the martyr of French Romanticism, who was there to study Simone Martini's lines. It was Géricault's mission to single-handedly arrest portraiture's inexplicable decline, and in circumspect little Alfred he immediately saw an exquisite model. He painted him standing on some rocks while a dry, warm foehn blew down from the Sienese slopes, flushing the boy's cheeks. (The portrait sitting in fact took place in his studio; the background came afterward.) The painting was ahead of its time in an era that tended to look on the young as nothing but adults in miniature: the boy Alfred stands out for the spirited look in his eye, his apparent cool indomitability.

A fateful encounter, it would seem, because when Dreux visited Géricault two months later in Paris he found that the master dealt not only in epic scenes of shipwrecks and hair-raising portraits of madmen, but also rather stripped-back animal pictures: portraits of horses, lions, and tigers, evincing the same penetrating eye as his portrayals of people. These images left an impression on Dreux, and when, years later, the Duke of Orléans wanted someone to paint his horses, he chose Dreux from among hundreds of candidates, thus sealing his reputation as the best equestrian painter in all of France. He came to the attention of King Louis-Philippe, who, in exile in England after the 1848 Revolution, invited him to cross the Channel several times on commissions. Dreux died at the age of fifty in Paris, of a liver abscess that had dogged him since his time in England, though a view prevailed in the salons that it was a saber wound from a duel with General Fleury, Napoleon III's aide-de-camp, after a disagreement the details of which the court-in-exile sought furiously to suppress.

What would the guests of the Errázuriz family have thought of these paintings? Would any of them have stopped to look at the Dreux? Or would their eyes have slipped over them the same as they did the beige wallpaper? I picture a group of them sitting around the table. The first course finished, the door opens and the head butler enters bearing the meat, served on a bed of boiled potatoes, a knob of butter and some fresh parsley on top; behind him comes one of the staff with the silver gravy boat, a hunting-horn motif etched along its sides. Someone mentions the treaty with Chile: war has been avoided. This is Señor Errázuriz's cue; in his capacity as ambassador, after all, he knows more than most. His wife, Josefina, smiles; a recent addition, she still thinks she's expected to show an interest in male conversation. She steals a look at the drawn face of the woman sitting on her right. She realizes—is alarmed to realize—that this will quite soon be her own face. She shakes out her hands, arresting the passage of time with a momentary drop in her blood pressure, which also has the effect of accentuating the whiteness of her skin. After dinner, the refuge of a game of whist. The only person to look at the painting is the older woman, Señora Alvear, once upon a time the famous soprano Regina Pacini: in fact her eye travels back and forth constantly between the deer in the picture, still alive, and the other one, dead and served to them in lean cuts. In the Renaissance-style parlor next door, a carved wooden clock chimes. The Señora Alvear shivers; a cold draft, she assumes. It has been some time now since she has known what it is that she feels.

Hunting scenes were quite common in Dreux's day, evocations of a sport that had been a class marker since the

Middle Ages, when the hunt became an elite pastime and often the only means of preparing men for war. An unintended by-product was that it gave the nobility a way of measuring itself—though only against itself. The first ever enclosures of forests and common land came about to enable exclusive access to big game. Commoners had to make do with birds and rabbits; bears, wolves, and deer became the landowner's right.

The Gothic art of the late Middle Ages emerged out of a meeting of Sienese and Flemish styles. The illustrated Book of Hours known as the *Très Riches Heures du Duc de Berry* is one of its best examples. The folio depicting the December "labors of the month"—activities undertaken by the duke's court and his peasants according to the time of year—shows hounds snapping at a boar's heels in a forest clearing, and could almost be a Dreux in miniature. It is likely that he saw the *Très Riches Heures* when he visited the Château de Chantilly with Napoleon III. The visual acuity he learned from Géricault was then combined with the languid, stylized approach of the manuscripts, and the resultant images, crammed with detail, had not a jot of empty space inside them: matter pervades every last inch.

Dreux pulses with atavistic symbolism: the struggle between good and evil, light and dark. The deer is about to die. One of the dogs sinks its fangs into the back;

another, a leg. The deer, on the verge of giving in, neck elaborately contorted, tongue out, is goggle-eyed with the same helpless astonishment as the hare described in Lampedusa's *The Leopard*: "Don Fabrizio found himself being stared at by big black eyes soon overlaid by a glaucous veil; they were looking at him with no reproval, but full of tortured amazement at the whole ordering of things." How well Lampedusa understood the unpredictability of events, their tendency to go full circle at the last, always leaving in their wake something akin to a glinting snail trail: ultimately ephemeral, certain to be lost in the mists of time.

Three years ago, a girlfriend of mine from university went for a walk around the edge of a hunting reserve in France. She was there visiting her Paris-based sister, a rising star at Lancôme who had met a Belgian millionaire and borne him two children. My friend was newly single and, being incapable of holding down a job, broke. But her sister bought her the plane tickets and insisted she come.

When she arrived, on a Friday morning, her sister announced that they had been invited to spend the weekend at a château in the country. They drove out in the afternoon despite dire weather warnings. An area of low pressure had come in and when they pulled up to the house the heavens opened. My friend found a bed and slept ensconced in a feather duvet until late the next morning. I picture her getting up and washing her face, and jumping when the gong was struck. She hurried downstairs. And saw out in the gardens twenty or so guests advancing zombie-like in the direction of a marquee in which a long table had been set for lunch. She fell in behind them. Her sister appeared a short while later and sat at the far end; the ski jacket of the previous night was gone, replaced by a green loden cape. Occasionally a gust of wind lifted a section of the marquee, giving a brief view of the rolling grounds, the lake with its thick covering of leaves, the enormous trees still dripping from the previous night's downpour. Some of the trees were so ancient that metal girders had been brought to prop up the branches, giving them a stooped look, like giants on crutches. The couple sitting next to her were both architects, and they talked for a while, but there was a chill to the northern air and at the first chance she dragged her chair over to a patch of sunlight to warm her bones. Coffee was still being served when she got up and said she needed to stretch her long legs—since the age of nine she'd had the spindly legs of a deer. One of the young men, French, offered to accompany her. He suggested they go to the end of the long allée and back.

They walked slowly. The path was muddy and the

wind rushed about in the casuarina trees. "We're bound to see some hares," said the young man. "It's the time of year for them." They came to the end of the allée and started back. In the distance, from some neighboring woods, a horn sounded. Someone calling the hounds in. Just then, my friend's boot became stuck in the mud. She strained to lift it out, but when her companion offered his hand, she waved him off impatiently: "I can manage." A second later a stray bullet hit her in the back, entering through one of her lungs.

She dropped to the ground; according to the Frenchman, her look was one of pure surprise. "Was that all?" it seemed to say. "Is that it?"

A month before, she and I had bumped into each other in the street. It had been ten years, and we stopped and caught up, or made a stab at it. She was attractive, thirty-five years old, and had got herself a new boyfriend and a job, too, in an auction house. She said she had been doing long hours for not very much money but, because she'd never felt the urge to have children, it didn't bother her. Whenever I think of her it's in the second when her boot sticks in the mud and she stops just where the bullet is about to strike. And I cannot tell what I should do with a death as ridiculous as hers, as pointless and hypnotic, nor do I know why I mention it now, though I suppose it's always probably the way: you write one thing in order to talk about something else.

THANK YOU, CHARLY

I woke to fog. And what a fog: as though a fat linen cloth had been draped across the world, giving a ghostly density to the view from my apartment window. The sun-blasted square, the headless statue of some worthy gentleman (the plaque was stolen a while ago, so everyone's forgotten who he is), the dogs sniffing the foot of the marble plinth, and their owners gathered in a circle, some with surgical masks, others covering their mouths with handkerchiefs. It was like one of those famous London fogs, but without the watery eeriness: a scratchy haze the color of unpolished granite. A mile-wide column of ash had entered the city from the west, blowing in from some meadow fires that had sprung up in the Delta. Emergency helicopters had been out for several days attempting to douse the flames. A few hours earlier, both of Buenos Aires's airports had been closed, and all road traffic was being diverted away from the city.

On the news it said there was nothing to worry about, that the carbon monoxide levels were low. That didn't stop me worrying about carbon monoxide levels. Any kind of pressure, it seems, and I come unstuck . . . I was on a ship once and began feeling seasick, my head spinning like a cheap umbrella in a storm. I went over to the railing and, though I did hear the other passengers call out that the waters were shark-infested, jumped straight in. When I feel wrong physically, any danger, however great, simply becomes unreal in comparison with my personal state. And now, now I had to escape this fog. I tried to convince my husband to leave the city with me; we could head south, the smoke was sure to clear at some point, we'd get a view of the sky again. Before I became pregnant I could be very persuasive, I'd do anything (anything) to get my way, but lately all my husband's replies had been starting with the word "no."

So I took the car and drove myself; my own private space to think. I put on my sunglasses to make it from the house to the car. I'd happily have donned a chador if I had owned one. I turned on the AC; bad idea: a blast of air like sandpaper hit me full in the face. After a brief coughing fit, I turned it off and headed south along Avenida Corrientes. I didn't know where I was going at first, but whenever I'm in survival mode like this I find myself drawn irresistibly to museums and galleries, like people running for air raid shelters in wartime. I remembered one on the other side of the city that I hadn't visited in a long time, which was strange given that the collection included work by one of my favorite painters. I'd been having to rest during the pregnancy, and was feeling rusty on my history of art, though I'm not sure that entirely explains why I talked to myself the entire way. I tried not to move my lips at traffic lights, so as not to alarm the other motorists. I told myself the story, or the bits I could remember, still coughing every now and then although I kept the windows up and the AC off. I was like a paleontologist climbing out of an excavation, bringing forth the final trio of bones she's been missing to piece together the creature.

Cándido López thought that in order to touch the heart of reality, it had first to be deformed. He studied under Ignacio Manzoni, who, convinced he saw signs of the true artist in López, suggested he go on a tour of Europe. Not having the money to do so, he set off around Buenos Aires Province instead, offering his services as a portrait painter, or he could do daguerreotypes if people preferred. He stopped in a place called Carmen de Areco, where nothing worth painting caught his eye except for a young American woman he met during carnival. She wore her hair in plaits, golden as wheat, and she also happened to be spoken for. López went on his way. An accounts book has survived from the time, and you can read all of his incomings and outgoings, town by town. Mercedes; Bragado; San Nicolás de los Arroyos. The last is where his records end, on April 12, 1865: we know that at some point that day Cándido López bought matches.

On the same day, President Mitre of Argentina refused permission to Solano López, the president of Paraguay, to sail a fleet past the river port of Corrientes and go to the aid of the Paraguayan Blanco Party. Solano López reacted angrily, capturing two Argentinian ships. In Buenos Aires the locals gathered outside the presidential palace to protest, chanting: "Death to the tyrant!" Argentina entered an alliance with Brazil and Uruguay, taking Paraguay as their common enemy, and the War of the Triple Alliance began. They put forward Solano López's dictatorial behavior as justification, but in war there are always two sides to the story—at least two sides. Control of the Paraguay River was the real prize. For the neighboring towns along this immense watercourse it was like being pitched into civil war, rather than a war between nations. Cándido

López, however, was pro-Mitre, and a porteño to boot, and when news of the hostilities reached him he went straight to the Guardia Nacional barracks in San Nicolás de los Arroyos to enlist. Some say he was compelled by a desire to put the American woman out of his mind, others that he had plans to set up as a war reporter. He took along a leather satchel full of notebooks and pencils. Manzoni's response was unequivocal: "With this you forsake any future as a painter."

CLEAN ME was written on the hoods of parked cars, and as the ash continued to drift lazily down, the world became less and less clearly defined. A painting in grisaille. The man in the car alongside mine was wearing a surgical mask and I, having been so terrified, suddenly felt a sensation of imperviousness, of utter immunity to the ash: do your worst, I thought. For a moment I forgot what I was doing and where I was going: so it seems to be anytime I experience happiness, it always has to be slightly to one side of reality. Some very faint jabs inside my belly brought me back to earth. I was much bigger than I had been just four weeks before. I still didn't know the baby's sex but, whatever it was going to be, it was that by definition—*going to be*. There, floating in its own private jacuzzi, it was in the best of all possible worlds. Future-bound, nothing more. I remembered the cloying song my mother used to sing to us at bedtime: "Qué será, será." I always found this both bewildering and depressing, mistaking it for a question, one that I was expected to answer, rather than a line about accepting your lot. How am *I* supposed to know what will be? I always wanted to shout. How I hated that song. I swear I ruined a childhood trying to come up with the right answer.

The *guardias* of San Nicolás ford the waist-high Batel River, wading on through the estuaries of eastern Argentina, watching for quicksand as they go. Dead bodies begin appearing four days in. Cándido López spends his free time sitting sketching the troops. "So much horror, it is difficult to look upon," he writes in his notebook after they camp in the vicinity of some emaciated children's corpses, so little flesh on their bones that the pyres refuse to light. All talk in the evenings ceases, and rather than falling asleep the men collapse into it: it would be quite possible for them to cross from sleep into death and not know it. One day Lieutenant Cándido López is called to General Mitre's tent. Mitre is deep in a translation of *The Divine Comedy*, but he has left his Italian–Spanish dictionary behind at their previous camp, and is looking for distractions while he waits for it to be brought. Looking over Cándido López's sketches, he says: "Look after these. History will have need of them one day." Then, putting the pictures to one side, he says: "Enough talk of you and me, let us discuss Dante." The dictionary never comes, and a number of hours later Mitre orders the advance on Curupaytí. Frustrated in his attempts to translate *The Inferno*, he chooses instead to perpetrate one of his own.

Later in the day, the Brazilian admiral, sensing rain, will advise against the attack. The Paraguayans have dug in: the trench is just over a mile long and lined with tree trunks, branches bristling forward like metal tines. The horn sounds and the Allies begin their advance, Cándido López running full tilt, eyes dead ahead, convinced that some invisible mantle is protecting him, until a grenade blows off his right hand—the one holding his saber aloft. He picks the weapon out of the tufty grass with his left and goes on, blood gushing from him; soon he begins to shake all over and, feeling nauseated, collapses in a crater.

Lying in the mud, he watches as a ladybug saunters along a blade of grass near to his face. A soldier, face bathed in blood, drops to the ground a few feet away. On the verge of losing consciousness, Cándido López drags himself to the camp at Curuzú. A medic does what he can to halt the gangrene, before deciding to cut off the hand. "Nothing for it." Weeks later, another amputation, this time above the elbow. The *guardias* of San Nicolás had set out with eight hundred volunteer soldiers, and eighty-three came back alive, including the One-Armed Man of Curupaytí. Cándido López is no good to the army anymore. The war goes on without him.

The fog grew thicker as I inched toward El Obelisco, the traffic semi-stationary. The man in the Fiat behind was blasting dementedly on his horn, as if he'd identified me as the root of all his life's problems. Can't you see it's the same for all of us? The ash had been causing mechanical failures across the city, and the traffic lights up ahead blinked amber without ever turning green or red. Brake or accelerate, I had no idea, always the way; everything ambiguous, everything admitting at least two interpretations. A Renault Megane, its driver wearing a surgical mask, tried to cut in off Humberto Primo: Over my dead body, mister! I put my foot down while honking on the horn, glaring across at him. Turning to look forward again, I found the exhaust pipe of a bus coming straight for my windshield. Before I knew it I'd gone into the back of the bus. The ash cloud also had strange acoustic properties: there was a jolting impact, but the sound of it came through muffled and indistinct.

•

Sir Richard Francis Burton wrote in a letter from an 1867 journey along the Paraguay River: "The ship went well, but our lives were literally in the hands of the drunken sots that drove her, and who passed their time draining the bottle or dancing bear-like to the colic-causing strains of travelling Italian zampognari." Not that he was afraid: he had explored Africa's inner reaches in search of the Nile's source, been on expeditions to uncover the fabled Icelandic sulfur mines, as well as translated *The Thousand and One Nights* and memorized the Koran; he was by now legendary in Britain for his capacity to blend in with the natives on his travels. But he was in Latin America as a British consul, and didn't need to disguise himself. He slept in the best hotels and rubbed shoulders with nobility, although his considerable beard failed to hide the scar on his cheek from a run-in with a Somali spearman. Burton was a man constantly at war with himself: part pure Victorian xenophobe, part "lover of all things heathen," as he put it. Just a fact of life for those of us who happen to exist at the interfaces between cultures.

A Paraguayan guide took him to see the battlefields. A sweet smell drifted across them, dust mixed with the scent of passion fruit in flower, and the Englishman sensed death in the air, the presence of "souls whose suffering is not ended." The pair went to leave, but the horses refused to take another step. The men dug in their spurs, but could not move the obstinate animals. Straight ahead of them, less than ten feet away, a skinny dog had stopped in their path. Red coat, black legs; in the fading light its silhouette had all the solidity of a mirage. Burton gave a friendly whistle—he had a way with dogs—but its only response was to raise its hackles and snarl.

At the end of the war Cándido López returns to Buenos Aires and takes a job in a shoe shop. One day the blond American woman he encountered in Areco comes in, though in fact her hair is brown: the blond plaits were a wig, part of an outfit for carnival. Her name is Emilia Magallanes, and she has recently been widowed, and Cándido López wastes little time before proposing. They decide to leave the city, going to a place called Baradero, halfway between Buenos Aires and San Nicolás de los Arroyos, where they set up as tenant farmers. In free moments Cándido López begins training his left hand. At first he produces nothing but unsightly scribbles: the right hemisphere of his brain needs dusting off. Once he has managed this, he turns to earlier sketches to begin a series of oil paintings depicting the Paraguay War. These together will eventually form his masterpiece, but they require a lot of work. The hell of the battlefields has stayed with him; he needs only a little solitude for it all to come flooding back. The fire and smoke pose him the greatest difficulties, but what painter can resist the impact of reds, oranges, and white emerging from a black horizon? In his work, though, fire always means dead men, and lots of them.

The new landowner comes to visit one day. He arrives not on horseback but in an automobile. His travels have taken him to Europe, and he's visited the Prado, the Louvre, the Uffizi, but nothing has prepared him for the pieces he finds on this farm. Cándido López always works in a format that is very wide but not correspondingly tall, and, stacked in a corner, the low, seemingly stretched images at first look dark—but when the painter brings them over to the window they shine. On the prompting of the landowner, he decides to exhibit. Dr. Quirno Costa makes arrangements at the local sports club, and twenty-nine works are put on show. "There, the history professors will have something to look at now," says Cándido López. The one or two reviews to appear in the newspapers concur: not bad for a one-armed man, and certainly of documentary value. Nonetheless they do not sell. What sell are his still lifes; these he carries out on commission, signing them *Zepol.*

On the twentieth anniversary of the Battle of Curupaytí, Cándido López offers his paintings to the state—for a fee. "I would donate them," he writes, "but

I am a very poor man." The government buys thirty-two paintings, which are handed over to the Museum of National History and end up in storage. One of the guards, nothing else to occupy him, spends the long hours staring at them as he sips his maté. His eye is particularly drawn to one called *Battle of Yataytí Corá*, though he thinks of it as "the black painting": it shows a field in Paraguay at night, fires raging. He sometimes thinks he glimpses white figures emerging from the charred forest in the background. He mentions this to the museum director in a hallway one day.

"You're telling me you've seen ghosts in the painting?" says the director.

"What I saw were white uniforms," says the guard.

Before embarking on the return river journey to Buenos Aires, Burton hears of a phalanstery in the middle of the jungle. "People live there who don't want war," say the peasant farmers. They are referring to a group of around two hundred deserters, from both sides, who have set up a utopian commune. They have women with them—prostitutes also tired of the war—and they all live together, at odds with the rest of the world but in harmony with nature. They claim that the *aguará guazú*, the maned wolf, comes out to watch over them at night. The Bordello of Chaco Plain, people call it. Its precise location is never established, nor what really goes on there, because no one who finds it ever comes back.

The museum director wants no loose talk on his watch. The following day, he arranges for the guard to be transferred to a local post office branch. Rumors of the white uniforms spread among the staff, and though they take care not to mention it in front of management, anytime they have to go down to the basement they always do so in pairs. Eighty years pass and Cándido López is never mentioned in art-historical discussions, until the critic Jose León Pagano includes him in his 1971 compendium *Argentinian Art*. Only then does Cándido López emerge from the basement.

No one on the bus even noticed, but I ended up with a smashed headlight. Could have been worse, I thought, as Lezama Park loomed up ahead, along with the Museum of National History, which had the look of a palace floating on clouds.

I'd had the constant sensation, for a while, that I was forgetting *something*. Since the conception, my brain had been leakier than a perforated hosepipe. When I walked past the two stone lions at the entrance, the same color as the ash, they eyed me sternly. I felt they could watch a person be impaled and still show no emotion. I ran a finger along one of their backs, coating my fingertip with gray. A sinking feeling came to me.

"The Cándido López paintings are up, aren't they?" I asked the ticket lady.

"No," she said, counting out my change with supreme impassivity (it was a donation). "They're being restored."

So that was why I had stopped coming.

"All thirty-two?"

My words hung in the air. The lady handed me my ticket. My condition wasn't going to make her budge. I remembered the sign from the conservators: they said it would take twelve months, but it had now been three years. Which meant there was nothing I wanted to see. I went in anyway.

I came out after a brief look around. I was feeling furious. Why did they have to take them all down at the same time? The thought of the restoration process was unnerving in the extreme, rendering the ash cloud a distant second. I simply couldn't believe it: the moment you get over one obstacle, up springs another. I found a bench and set my handbag down as a cushion. There was a fair in the park below, stalls selling handicrafts, Justin Bieber T-shirts, DVDs, little multicolored ponies, and people milled around, appearing out of the fog, disappearing into it, slightly like a B movie with cheap special effects. I was lowering myself onto my handbag (an undertaking) when I heard something go crunch, and remembered my glasses were inside. I got up and fished them out, first one arm, then the other: they reminded me of the legs of an Amazonian mosquito, and something about this just broke my heart. I felt suddenly felled, everything was a disaster, no more trying to deny it: I simply wasn't cut out for life. I was an army of one, and as the enemy bore down, when they were right on top of me, only then would I realize I'd forgotten my bayonet.

Mitre had promised: "In twenty-four hours we will be in barracks; in two weeks the campaign will begin; in three months, we take Asunción." The war lasted nearly five years, and more than 50,000 were killed. When the troops returned to Buenos Aires, a yellow fever epidemic ensued. The aristocratic families moved to the north of the city, abandoning their mansions in the south, many of which were converted into boardinghouses in the following months. A number of these families also acquired land in Paraguay for next to nothing.

Three decades ago my husband went to live on one of those parcels of land. He went with his first wife, Cecilia, and her brother Charly. The idea was to work the land, though it was also an escape from the claustrophobia of late-1970s Buenos Aires under the junta. Charly was the moving spirit, the dreamer. "Enough of this shithole," he said. "Let's have our very own Woodstock, Guaraní-style!" They went to a place called La Serena, deep in the jungles of Paso Curuzú, on land owned by Charly and Cecilia's father, Franio, a man whose gaze would darken by degrees as he proceeded to drink his daily succession of whiskeys. Franio was half-Paraguayan, half-Argentinian, and his father had been minister for the economy in the government of Alfredo Stroessner. He had inherited thousands of hectares in San Pedro Department, but was no enthusiast when it came to agriculture. The trio set up in the main house, a single-floor building with whitewashed walls and a veranda held up by a colonnade of quebracho trees. The walls were thick enough that the windowsills served as seats, and the master bedrooms had all been built overlooking the vast *finca*.

For the two men, both under twenty-two, it was like a game. In the mornings they went out riding. They took bags of salt with them in their panniers, brought in any bulls that had crossed onto the mountainside, and checked on how the kikuyu grass was growing, the aggressive *Pennisetum clandestinum* that Franio had planted for pasture. In the surrounding jungle—vast tracts that could be crossed only by plane—myrtle, the white-leaved *inga* shrub, and papaya grew unchecked.

My future husband and Charly had been friends since childhood. They both played the guitar, both wrote songs, and they fantasized about one day setting up a band. Marrying Charly's sister had been the most manly way of sealing their friendship. In the photos from that time my husband wears flares, a guitar at his shoulder; Charly stands beside him in a tie-dye T-shirt. Their hair is long—my husband's chestnut brown, Charly's a deep black. They're constantly laughing, the kind of laughter that shows the canines—they remind me of hyenas. I once asked my husband what the joke had been. "Couldn't tell you," he said. "We were stoned pretty much twenty-four seven."

They all sat down together for dinner one night at La Serena. Franio had arrived in the afternoon: his first appearance since they had been there. He bore the gift of a very large bottle of whiskey, so large it was held inside a hinged metal contraption that enabled you to pour without pulling a muscle. A gift that was also a way of saying "mine." "Manna from heaven," he said, setting it down on the table. "None of that horse piss the English drink at five in the afternoon." My husband had met his father-in-law only twice, owing to the long periods Franio spent in Europe; his children said he always had a mistress with him on his travels, but the mistresses changed so frequently they never got a name. The last time they had seen each other was at the wedding reception; the party lasted until dawn, and at some point my husband went to the toilet and found Franio in there. "You want to be very careful with what isn't yours," Franio said, eyes front at the adjacent urinal. My husband kept his eyes fixed on the white tiles above his urinal, and was able to piss only once Franio had left.

After dinner in La Serena, Cecilia went off to clean the dishes and the men made themselves comfortable out on the veranda. They left the lights off to avoid insects. The crickets chirred, lizards darted around under the seats, bats swooped overhead, and the dogs slunk to and fro, panting in the airless night. They were country dogs. Nobody claimed ownership of them, and they recognized no masters. Franio had started drinking early—"Wouldn't want to overheat," he'd said—and went on pouring himself glass after glass in the darkness. He had his own glass, though my husband says a pitcher would be a better description, and he was knocking whiskeys back like aspirin. My husband drank his over ice; Charly was teetotal, wary of alcohol as children of bad drinkers always are, but that night he had poured himself a glass for the first time. Two fingers of whiskey. He was always on edge around his father.

The fan above them spun around on its highest setting. Serú Girán played on the little Sony cassette player, though Franio soon asked the boys to switch it off. They had little in common, and the conversation inevitably turned to the farming. Charly and my husband had been finding the going harder than they had expected. My husband thought pigs might be an idea. Franio, reaching for another drink, said nothing. "You can do well out of them," insisted my husband, making his case, using terminology learned during the months he'd spent there. He mentioned the spike in beef prices, and talked about exporting to Russia. Franio, staring into his glass, moved his head from side to side. Moths flew repeatedly into the mosquito screen covering the windows behind them, trying to reach the lights in the living room, as though pleading to be let in.

"Didn't you tell this guy nobody tells me what to do?" said Franio. Though addressing Charly, he was looking straight at my husband.

"We'd need time, obviously . . ." said my husband, but suddenly Franio was on his feet and had taken his pistol out from under his guayabera.

Charly sat stock still. As did my husband; he looked at the gun, which in the low light seemed to dance a little waltz on the air before him.

"You little pricks," said Franio. "I'm the boss around here. If you don't like it, the gate's open."

His hands were shaking. He took a step back, so that they could barely make him out, but the anger in his voice remained all too clear. The crickets had fallen silent. Charly twirled a cigarette between his fingers and kept his eyes on the ground.

"And what's up with you? Missing a bone or something? Look at me when I talk!"

They both knew the myth about the Paraguayans lacking a bone, this being why they didn't hold their heads up—the reason for a purported submissiveness.

"Don't get heavy, right? I know, I know, everything's *cool.* Think you've got it made, don't you, you and that guitar of yours are going places?"

Then, finger still on the trigger, he began talking in Guaraní. His voice changed, grew thick, and as it resounded in the darkness it was as though everything had disappeared and it was just Franio, talking to himself, or talking to someone inside his head—deep, deep inside. Then there was a howl and Franio whirled around.

"Who's out there?" Then, to his son, in his normal voice again: "Light, fuck sake, shine a light!"

Charly snatched up the storm lamp and lit it. The flame jumped up with a hiss, blinding them all momentarily and illuminating the cocked heads of the dogs—all looking in the direction of a tree-covered knoll a little way in the distance. There was nothing there. My husband got a view of the gun, and saw that it was a Parabellum. A detail he always includes at this point in the story: the Parabellum was a German pistol, more commonly known as a Luger, after its inventor, Georg Luger. But the name Luger had chosen came from a maxim in Latin: *Si vis pacem, para bellum*: If it is peace you want, prepare for war.

"Shine it that way," ordered Franio, lurching off the veranda, past the dogs and away in the direction of the knoll. He suddenly seemed not to have a care in the world, and tottered off with the dogs sniffing after him. A hammock had been slung between a couple of the trees, and he subsided into it, gun on his stomach, the other hand hanging down. He stroked the head of one of the dogs, until eventually his hand hung slack as a bunch of bananas. His snoring rang out as the million-starred sky looked on blithely, quite indifferent to terrestrial concerns. Charly went back into the house. My husband put out the lamp and sat a little while longer. One by one the crickets started up again, until the night was full of their song once more.

The next morning, straight from the shower, his wet hair swept back, Franio put on an exaggerated air of innocence. Helping himself to a third cup of coffee, he popped a succession of *chipá* rolls into his mouth and cracked jokes, most of which were about Paraguayan women cuckolding their men. My husband sat at the table and listened. Franio was due to leave shortly for Asunción in his private jet: he was the pilot. My husband needed to go to the city as well but said nothing. He would rather the seven-hour journey in the back of the milk truck than be shut in a cockpit with his father-in-law. Charly wasn't there to say goodbye; he had gone out riding early.

The situation soon turned sour. Franio had seen the obvious: they were too soft, and too hippyish, to keep the place in check. They also began to squabble, and Charly getting high on a daily basis didn't help. My husband threw in the towel at the end of the year and went back to Buenos Aires. Cecilia went to Asunción. Charly stayed on at La Serena, and Franio began to visit more frequently, which troubled my husband. He called Charly up to convince him to come back too, but he said he'd grown to like it there. Like the *aguará guazú*, he had found somewhere in the undergrowth to hide, a place where he and his demons could have it out.

A year after they had separated, and nearly ten years after they first met, Cecilia rang my husband from Asunción. Franio had died a month before, she said, and she was worried about her brother. He had been found wandering around naked on the mountainside a few days after the death, and it was now ten days since she'd heard from him. "Even in his really bad periods, he always calls every two or three days." She said she would have asked the local farmers, but she was concerned that people would start to talk. Would he go, please? She begged him; the family would cover his costs.

My husband arrived at La Serena at night. The beams of the car headlights swung across oranges rotting on the branches. Weeds were growing up between the veranda flagstones, and the jungle seemed poised, ready to take back this strip of land that men had toiled so long to clear. The only people left were a handful of locals; he found them perched in the palm trees in the moonlight, cutting down the leaves they used to thatch their huts. Nobody had seen anyone come out of the main house for days, but neither had they felt much like going inside. My husband crossed the veranda and pushed open the door. It was the same inside as when he had left: the smell of whiskey and ash, the armchair decorated with cigarette burns, and the Sony cassette player positioned next to the fireplace. He called out, and got no answer, though when he strained to listen he could make out a low wheezing sound somewhere inside the house. He established that it was coming from the main bedroom, the door to which he found ajar. Looking in, he found Charly sitting on the stripped wooden floor, the strings of his guitar wrapped around his neck, chewing on something. Moving closer, my husband saw cassette tapes scattered around, the tape unspooled: this was what Charly was chewing. My husband looked into his eyes. They sparkled but at the same time looked vacant, like those of a stuffed animal.

Charly was taken to Asunción and committed. For the next few years he was in and out of various rest clinics.

Every now and then the phone will ring in the middle of the night. I happened to be awake the last time it did, having been trying to get comfortable in bed for hours, my mind buzzing, and my bladder, with the baby pushing on it, forcing me to make several trips to the toilet; the due date was a few weeks away. My husband opened his eyes and immediately shook his head. He knew who it would be. I picked up, and was greeted by Charly's slurred voice. I had only ever heard it at this hour; perhaps that accounts for it seeming so distinctive. Music was playing in the background.

"I'm listening to the record that shithead next to you made. I know he's there, and I know he's ignoring my calls. Know what, though?" He laughed. "I don't care if he doesn't want to speak to me."

"He's fast asleep, Charly. Bombs could be going off."

I'd usually cut the conversation short, always feeling like an intruder in their relationship, but now a nighttime confidant was exactly what I needed. I'd never met Charly in person, we were two voices in the night: perfect for the speaking of truths.

"You know you married a fucking madman, right? I always told him he had a screw loose."

I smiled. Charly knew my husband in ways I didn't. He started talking about when they were young, the time they spent in Paso Curuzú, and there was something comforting in hearing it; no bitterness in his voice. Then, suddenly, he said he had to go:

"Doubtless you won't believe me, but someone here needs the phone."

He was right, I didn't believe him. A vague stab at politeness as he went to hang up, leaving a woman alone with her insomnia. It was then that he asked:

"Things okay there?"

"Sure," I said. "We're pregnant."

I tried to sound happy, radiant even, like the women in magazines. But I wasn't fooling Charly. Eventually I gave in:

"I don't know, Charly. I've been feeling like I might not be ready."

Then, out of the oceanic night, I heard him sigh and say "Little lady"—final proof that he didn't know me, because truly I was far from little. But I liked the way he said it, and decided not to correct him. And, as though he knew, he said it again:

"Little lady . . . None of us is ever prepared for anything. That's what's so funny, right?"

He laughed to himself, a flash of teeth in the darkness. "What do I know, but anyway that's how it seemed to me then."

He didn't say when he was referring to, or where, but something told me he meant during his time in the jungle. He hung up, and I sat thinking about what he'd said. His meaning wasn't entirely clear, a little like if you ever read your horoscope or look at a fortune cookie, but it didn't matter, he had still given me a lift. As the first rays of sunlight began to filter through the shutters, and with the receiver resting on my belly, I murmured, "Thank you, Charly." It was then, hearing myself speak, that I remembered this was the catchphrase of the three heroines in my favorite TV series as a child. I'd tell him, I thought, the next time he called. Then again, I wasn't sure if Charly would know what I was talking about, being that much older than me. A different generation entirely.

THE ENCHANTMENT OF RUINS

You spent the first half of your life rich, the second poor. Not in penury, but always needing to be careful, always forgoing possible little treats, and often being forced to borrow when unanticipated costs arose. Hence the Silver Spoon syndrome that has always marked you out: the indestructible sensation that *the money will come from somewhere.* It isn't that you delude yourself into thinking the coffers are overflowing, rather it's like an unshakable inner security—yet another illusion, of course, only in your case a very convincing one. You belong to a class generations deep in the assumption that there will be a hot meal on the table every night. A blessing, very much so, but also something of a curse: never experiencing hunger has made you idle. (The reverse happens with rich people who grew up poor; it is a commonplace that the cold and the constant sensation of *there never quite being enough* enter a person's bones, like a never-ending toothache.) You have the ability to get by on rice for long periods, partly because bad fortune never seems set to last; a better time is sure to come. And you do always try to steer clear of another of the pathologies that attends comfortable upbringings: Poor Little Rich Girl syndrome. That, to you, is not to be entertained.

Yeats spoke of the Celtic twilight, and warded off his melancholy by pouring himself into Greek translations. Dead languages have never been your forte, but you have other things, a manicure being the cheapest option you've come up with to keep your darkness at bay. And in general it's worked, helping you to stay present, restricting your focus to that tiny portion of your self. Nowadays, if you let yourself become distracted, if there is some pause in the application of the nail varnish, why lie? You're the very first to let ruins enchant you. Some days you are liable to be devastated by a broken nail, or a cuticle that's ever so slightly too big, or the nail varnish chipping; and cracks suddenly appear in the dam that keeps all of your sadness in check.

•

Save for a few pieces of paper scurrying along the pavements like frightened animals, Avenida Corrientes is deserted. Tears stream down your face. A Siberian wind is blowing, and you and your daughter are huddling close as you advance along the street, when a vision presents itself: out of the sewers come princes with crooked crowns, beaten-up-looking fairies, queens with dirty stoles, pusses in tatty leather boots, wicked stepmothers in bunched-up dresses; into the vacuum of the abandoned metropolis these characters rush, apparently themselves startled at their reflections in the windows of bars and shops. They proceed to a corner up ahead, where they assemble and begin proffering flyers for a play—with a medieval theme. As they pass, you notice a half-built house. It has scaffolding and security netting all around it. Nothing resembles a ruin more than a building under construction, you think to yourself, before catching sight of three young farm girls skipping around among the rubble and building materials. You are immediately reminded of a painting by Hubert Robert. You smile, the involuntary smile usually prompted only by the sight of a helium balloon drifting up past the never-ending cables and utility poles of a city sky. Hubert Robert always makes you think of your mother. He was the only painter the two of you could agree about.

•

You've only ever seen one Hubert Robert in the flesh, at the National Museum of Decorative Arts. It wasn't so much on display as hidden away in a tiny passageway on the third floor. The canvas is tall and narrow, and depicts a group of young people at play in the ruins of a Greek temple. Anywhere you look in the painting, at the crumbling temple, at the withered tree, or at the starving mule, everything points to endings, or *the* end. The only distraction, and a momentary one at that, is the young people's game. Like the dog that, after the bombing of Berlin, emerged from the rubble, dug up a bone and played with it for a short while, and when it saw a tank rumbling past at top speed threw itself under the tracks.

The aesthetic of decay was not invented by Hubert Robert, but he does represent its apotheosis. Ruins were a fashionable subject in late-eighteenth-century art, as he'd learned during his traineeship with René Slodtz. It was under Slodtz's tutelage that he developed a liking for decorative garden follies—all those columns, pagodas, and obelisks. It didn't matter which culture or period in history they belonged to, as long as they were old and crumbling, and above all a fabrication. Every aristocratic residence, to be worthy of the name, had to have one or two mock ruins strategically scattered throughout its grounds. The most extreme cases attempted to generate a sensation of full-blown catastrophe, with fire-spitting grottos, volcanoes on the verge of erupting, and even sudden torrents of rain.

The mock ruin was seen as a way of establishing a lost link with antiquity; it was no coincidence that the trend arose on the eve of the Industrial Revolution. With the move away from nature came an exaggerated melancholy for all that was lost, and the rich learned to delight in their sadness. Imagine a group of people with a lot of free time on their hands wandering around among Roman plinths, musing on glories past. Sometimes the follies functioned as memento mori: the owners of the property could go for a stroll in the grounds and, coming upon a tumble-down plinth or statue, allow themselves to experience despair: they, too, would have it all taken from them one day! "A stairway, leading to no palace at all! Look upon these ruins and experience the very vertigo of life," wrote Charles de Brosses upon seeing the intentionally unfinished marble structure in Madame de Neuilly's gardens. "I cannot say what the place was like, only that this cut-off staircase was the most beautiful thing in all of architecture and brought me as much if not more satisfaction than the sight of a building, full and entire." Sometimes these extravagances fulfilled practical demands as well: in 1740, Lord Belvedere had a Gothic abbey built in his grounds, and it was so dilapidated that the slightest gust would topple stones from the apices and flying buttresses. The abbey, also known as the Jealous Wall, blocked out the view of the home of Belvedere's younger brother, a raffish androgyne with long ringletted hair whom Belvedere suspected of having wooed his wife.

On a winter's night when you were ten, there was a fire in the study at your home. One of your brothers had been poring over his schoolbooks late into the night, forgot to put out the little brazier when he went to bed, and an armchair cushion caught fire. You were woken by the smell of burning, and went out to find smoke pouring from the study. Your screams woke the house, your brother appearing with a bucket and your father going out to the balcony to call down for help. You went looking for your mother, an involuntary reflex in you: anytime you felt in danger, it was to her you turned. But though you went around all of the bedrooms, she was nowhere to be found.

The firemen took axes to the front door and, possibly confused by the zebra carpet, the stuffed quetzal birds, and the Louis XVI chairs with lion-paw feet, hacked and slashed their way into the junglelike interior of the apartment. The family was evacuated down the servants' stairs, to be met by a small crowd of neighbors in the entrance hall. Your mother was yet to be found and you were horribly worried but didn't know who to tell: anyway, everyone had their hands full rushing around seeing to things. A neighbor brought you a cup of tea and, lifting it to your mouth and taking a reviving sip, you saw, through the steam, your mother out on the sidewalk. Barefoot, she was wearing what she would have referred to as her "pretties": a white camisole, with a single button, the wrong one, done up, so that her stomach and her bloomers were on show. The porter had earlier seen her run off in the direction of the U.S. embassy, which was a block away. You buried your face in your hands. A few nights later you wrote in your diary: "Mother in her bloomers. Somber sight."

You should have guessed. Anytime anything went wrong your mother would hurry off to the embassy, the small mansion that, before it became the embassy, had been her grandmother's home. She was five years old when the property was sold, and found it so traumatic that she was from then on incapable of letting anything go; normal houses have one sofa, maybe two, but your mother had seven, most of them stacked up in the bedrooms you and your siblings slept in as children. In the closet of what used to be your bathroom there is a pile of Sotheby's catalogues dating back to 1972, the shelves bowed under their weight. One day a triple mirror that had been leaning against some bookshelves came crashing down on top of her; she said afterward that she had been trying to find a book to lend the porter. Which book? *Los que mandan*

(The Ruling Class), by José Luis de Imaz; it was a lifelong obsession of hers to disseminate the "correct" history of our country. She was stuck beneath the mirror for half an hour, until the maid came in and heard her shouting. She was unhurt. It has occurred to you that, toppling furniture allowing, your mother will one day create her own Hubert Robert landscape. Guided tours of her apartment will be provided, foreigners will queue up along Avenida Libertador, eyes fixed on the third floor of the building, where, behind those very tall double-glazed windows, not a speck of dust is allowed to settle on the ruins of the Argentinian nobility.

When he became tired of imitations, Hubert Robert went in search of real ruins. He visited Naples, produced studies of Herculaneum and Pompeii, sketched the palace at the Villa d'Este in Tivoli, and ended up creating images that were an exact likeness of antiquity, only shorn of antiquity's confidence in the future. The trick was to aspire to the greatness of Rome while at the same time acknowledging its irremediable lostness. Ruins seemed to him a kind of meditation on a society that no longer saw itself living in a time of continuity, but rather a time of contingency. It was a vision that nonetheless lacked the intensity of Piranesi or the gravitas of Poussin. He came back to Paris with a gift from a Roman client: a fourteenth-century church lectern in the shape of an eagle, the slanted reading board resting on outstretched wings. He put it in the entranceway to his workshop, using it as a coat stand, and every time he left, hanging his painting smock on it as he passed, it gave him the sensation of embracing success. Hordes of customers would crowd at the door to his workshop, all of them eager to own a landscape by Hubert Robert, all dying to have one of the ruins pieces hanging in their homes: these had become the most effective *pièce de conversation* of the day, the perfect stimulus anytime the talk began to flag. Quite without meaning to, Robert had channeled the zeitgeist.

The fire damage was minimal. Your mother's flight to the embassy was never spoken about. Whenever you remember it, a part of you feels embarrassed, but another part smiles. A slave to convention most of the time, your mother is also capable of surprising outbursts of originality. She was driving you to school one day and you noticed that she had all the car mirrors pointed at her—and, troubled, pointed it out. "Oh, darling," she said, "nobody actually *uses* those things. They're only good for checking your makeup. Anyway, I can sense it intuitively if anything's about to hit me. Intuition's far more useful than eyesight." In such moments, you glimpse something that redeems her in your eyes, something to make you lament that her craziness has never fully prevailed over her constant tendency to conform.

The works of Hubert Robert are like a premonition: a painter seeing what's on the horizon and transferring it to the canvas in loose, open-ended brushstrokes. He painted quickly. A Russian prince who had been vying for ownership of one of his pieces said: "He wants the money to come in at the same pace he works at. He dashes off pictures as quickly as writing letters." And the unfinished impression of his paintings was also appropriate to their subject, as though an earthquake had struck while Robert was at the easel, forcing him to abandon the job. When the world is precarious, his paintings seem to say, the idea of finishing anything stops making sense. "The world was . . . unlasting, what could be forever? or only what it seemed? rock corrodes, rivers freeze, fruit rots . . . and who is lonelier: the hawk or the worm?" wrote a twelve-year-old Truman Capote on the bank of a swampy Alabama river.

Robert was a celebrated painter, universally recognized, when one day all his good luck ran out. Each of his children died in quick succession: Gabriel, Adelaide, Charles, and Adèle. Napoleon came to power soon after, and he was expelled from the Académie and imprisoned at Saint-Lazare (along with the Marquis de Sade). He avoided the guillotine because of an administrative error (another prisoner was killed in his place). After his release, he was employed as an architectural advisor in the building of the Louvre, for which he was paid a token salary, barely enough to live on. He went to his studio late one night to do some work on the plans and, coming into the small, cramped space, tripped. This is how I imagine Hubert Robert's death: brained by his eagle lectern. He was seventy-five years old, nine months in arrears on his rent, and quite alone in the world.

When you turned fourteen, your parents went to see your outcast older brother in San Francisco and came back with a gift for you. As always around that time, their presence was nothing but an irritant. It was as though you constantly expected your *real* family to step forward at some point and gather you up. You came in to find your mother unpacking. She pointed to a plastic bag: "There you go, Little Miss Crazy. It's for you." There was a Golden Gate Bridge snow globe inside. When you shook it the tiny flecks of snow came swirling up, tumbling and swirling before falling so gently, so comfortingly, that you felt as though snowfall like that could heal any kind of pain.

With it was a card, a page hastily torn from a notebook. In sloping, barely legible handwriting, it said:

> *We are losing men*
> *And all our ammunition is gone*
> *But they don't know that*
>
> —FEDERICO WILLIAMS

There has been a refrain from your mother and those around her, ever since you can remember: "Any minute now, this country is going up in flames." Thirty years on, they're still awaiting the conflagration. She checks on a weekly basis whether her granddaughter has a passport, there obviously being "no future for her here." Obviously. When she talks like this it puts you in mind of the "Hateful Poet" Cecco Angiolieri, whom Marcel Schwob says felt black for no other reason than that his father was white. Your daughter doesn't have a passport, and yours expired eons ago. You like the neighborhood you're living in, love it in fact, and you don't feel as though you'll ever leave. Even if your mother does thinks it borders barbarian lands.

Over the years, the fights have grown less fierce. Both of you are older and more tired now, and each argument comes to resemble the latest instalment in a comedy: one recently found you pursuing her through a hallway in her house reading aloud from an Irène Némirovsky book: "In the rare moments when she displayed any maternal affection, pressing her daughter to her breast, her nails almost always scratched Hélène's bare arm or face." Your mother, showing uncustomary agility as she tried to get away from you, muttered: "All this *muck* you read, girl!" The only thing ever to bring the two of you together, the only bridge, is Hubert Robert. And it is the briefest of moments, a burst of light illuminating the relationship you could have enjoyed—had either of you been willing to concede a little, had you resisted being consumed by these roles you play. But it's difficult to go back now. In her eyes you'll always be the one who blew your good fortune, silly little girl, silly self-appointed pariah. This is your choice, you snap; you happen to like living in no-man's-land. And that one day you're going to build your own house using her furniture—after you've smashed it all to pieces.

SEPARATE WAYS

During a particularly harrowing period in my adolescence, when I was not yet an adult but no longer a child either, and all too obviously a conundrum for every single person who encountered me, my family and I moved in with my grandmother. The official line was that the apartment needed redecorating after the fire. But a year later, when we moved back, everything was just as we had left it. Unless it was the kind of decoration job that meant leaving a pile of charred magazines on the table in the study. I never found out the real reason for that year away, but then whose life doesn't contain uncertainties? Some details are lost to time, and in fact it's for the best. To ever feel that you understand anything only means that your mind has turned rigid.

My grandmother lived in an art deco bunker, with a spiral staircase whose handrail curled around on itself like a question mark. The garden took up half a block, and had a sixty-foot swimming pool that years later went on to be sold to the university, covered over, and turned into a squash court. The servants' entrance (there was a small army of them) was set into the wall at the bottom of the garden, concealed by a climbing pepper vine. A door I was forbidden to use, on the basis that—according to Mama—the neighbors might see me and think I was the maid's daughter.

The only times I broke the rule were on the one or two occasions I accompanied my father to Amuchástegui's studio. It was quicker than going out the front door and all the way back around the side of the garden. Amuchástegui painted animals and lived in a crumbling Victorian house. My father went to see him not so much to invest in his work as for a release. He would sit in an apparently ahistorical threadbare armchair and drink tea out of a jam jar, and, as he sat surveying Amuchástegui's mildew-speckled paintings, would begin to resemble a man very much like himself, except one that was at ease.

While we were living at my grandmother's, my friend Alexia stayed over a few times, and one day when we had nothing else to do my father suggested a visit to the studio. Amuchástegui wasn't usually the most scintillating company but that afternoon he was in high spirits, far friendlier than I had ever seen him. Without anyone asking, he showed us—though really I think it was just Alexia he was showing—his technique, which involved the use of a very fine sable brush that he kept in a jar of turpentine. I remember the smell of the turps: so strong it reached into the inner recesses of your skull. When we came to leave, also apropos of nothing, or, more probably, of men's innate competitiveness in the company of women, my father took out his checkbook and bought a painting of a cat perched in a tree. Actually, said Amuchástegui, it was a wildcat. That was odd, I remember thinking, it didn't look very wild to me. Its ocher-and-black fur was painted hair by hair, with an attention to detail that made my head spin. Hyperrealism, my father called it later that day as he hung the piece in the study at my grandmother's. Alexia declined to comment—she who had an opinion on just about everything. But three years after that, when I convinced her to come to the National Museum of Fine Arts with me one day, we saw the Foujita self-portrait for the first time: that lithe Japanese painter with his sly-looking cat, rendered in a series of rapid black brushstrokes. Alexia caught my eye, and I knew exactly what she was thinking, our telepathy being fairly well established by then: that the one my father had bought looked positively mummified by comparison.

We called each other soul sisters and snobbishness became our shared defense mechanism, partly because we were both naturally reticent and partly as a heightened mode of sincerity. At times she was my other half, my better half, and at times my own private Sherpa. I went to a private school in the north of the city, she to a school for dropouts in the center. The syllabus at mine was full of gaping holes and, apart from a good grasp of English, I came away knowing just about nothing. At hers, on the other hand, they seemed to be taught everything of any importance, and in depth. She had twin older brothers who were both rockers, and their black sleeveless Ramones T-shirts made my brothers' yellow Lacoste polos look like enemy fatigues. Alexia exposed me to many of the things that would go on to be the fuel in my life; at thirteen she took me to see *A Clockwork Orange* in a dive cine club in Abasto; six months later she lent me J. D. Salinger's *Nine Stories*, a copy that looked more dog-chewed than dog-eared; and it was with her that I first listened to Sumo, on a pirate cassette tape her brothers had recorded at Einstein's. At fifteen we plundered her father's bar: half a finger of whiskey each, three cubes of ice, up to the top with soda water, and still our tongues grew thick and heavy with each sip. At sixteen we were the divinely appointed rulers of our neighborhood, constantly stoned, constantly traversing Buenos Aires (in taxis) in search of the perfect party. Of course we'd fall out, and when we did we'd go our separate ways for a while until one of us finally gave in and picked up the phone. And then it would be back to our customary idyll, long periods of mutual veneration, she making an Egyptian cat of me and me of her. When our relations approached the summit of spiritual communion again, when our shared understanding became such that each could hop inside the other's head at will, that was a sign that we were due another bad patch.

"If my mom calls, tell her I'm sleeping at your house tonight," she declared over the phone one Saturday morning, before promptly hanging up. I next heard from her late on the Sunday evening: "Been away." I never understood, and never felt like asking, why parts of Alexia were always out-of-bounds to me. I later learned that she had gone to take ayahuasca in a quinta out in Moreno. I was never invited along. She liked keeping me on the periphery of her life. She liked making me feel like I didn't have whatever was needed to get close to her.

•

"How lovely he is!" sigh the women on board the *Nishimaru* as the Japanese man, eyes lanceolate like bamboo leaves, comes by. He is wearing a plum-colored suit, on his head is a *salacot* like that of an intrepid British explorer in tropical lands, the whole outfit topped off by an emerald necklace. This is one of the many jaw-dropping outfits he likes to sport. He was born in Tokyo in 1886, across from the Shin-Ohashi bridge, at a sharp, choppy bend in the Sumida River. His father was a general in the imperial army, and he inherited from him a taste for military theatricality; from his mother, who died when he was five, a sense of detachment. But it is the thought of Europe that sparks his artistic ambition. When the Meiji Restoration sees Japan open up to foreign influence, and Western images begin to circulate, the aspiring painter of the floating world is dazzled by the work of the cutting-edge European artists of the day. "Impossible to live on an island without becoming insular!" he writes in his diary. He comes dashing along the snow-covered streets of Tokyo, a huge book of Cézanne prints under his arm; and later, at dinner, is to be seen poring over the images, rice from his bowl spilling across Mont Sainte-Victoire. Tsuguharu Fujita is twenty-six when he books a passage on the *Nishimaru*. His destination is Paris. He does not yet know that Paris is the perfect place to reinvent oneself. Or perhaps he knows it very well, perhaps that's exactly what he's hoping for.

•

At the time when taxis ruled the roads in Buenos Aires, the taxi firms came up with the CTC, or Constant Traveler Coupon, which took the form of a green cardboard loyalty card. You earned points with each journey, and could eventually claim a dinner for two in a restaurant of your choice. We always went to Habibi, a little Arab place in Villa Crespi; Alexia liked anywhere that seemed exotic, and I never said no to anything with a touch of the decadent. We invariably reserved the table in the corner at the back, which had a red tablecloth and a rusty old hookah pipe serving as a vase.

"So bored," Alexia said to me one night as the resident belly dancer sashayed before the next table along. "Buenos Aires is so *tedious*."

This was a fairly constant refrain from Alexia. Why bother answering?

"You think you're so cool," she said. "Don't you want to travel, see the world?"

"Not really. My Chinese horoscope's the dog. Melancholic, not ambitious."

"But don't you feel suffocated?"

There had been one winter when I felt suffocated. I know it was winter because *Holiday on Ice* had come to Buenos Aires, and for the first time an open audition had been announced. "It isn't art, it's a circus," said my mother. "At least set your sights on the Bolshoi." There ended my career as an ice-skater, before it had begun. Whenever the oracle spoke, I paid attention, however grudgingly; my mother had a proven ability to see into the future, and everyone in the family followed her prognostications to the letter. She believed herself to be a witch, a real witch, because her birthday was on Halloween. (I, in grotesque contrast, was born on Christmas Day, which by the same logic should have made me a saint but instead meant I just resented my birthday, never getting to be center stage.) To my mother, attending a *Holiday on Ice* casting would be to join the legions of underachievers jostling to see who could be the biggest failure of all. An idea that, deep down, I quite liked: the perfect excuse to indulge my congenital laziness. Odd, but there are some battles you prefer to lose. Not for nothing did it say on my seventh grade school report: "When she applies herself, she excels. Only she hardly ever applies herself." I had come to the conclusion that it was more elegant to be on the losing side. Alexia, however, constantly managed to pour cold water on such thinking. She wanted to climb the highest heights, and quickly.

The *Nishimaru* docks in London, and Fujita, to whom all cities are alike, disembarks. When he learns of his error, he doesn't let it worry him, and soon finds work as a tailor at Selfridges. Though a dab hand with a pair of scissors, he quickly tires of the English capital: "I did not leave one island only to end up on another." On arrival in Paris, he takes a hovel room in Cité Falguière, a tiny cat-infested cave. He becomes friendly with his downstairs neighbor, an Italian artist who tries to pay his rent in paintings. "The only thing these are good for is fixing the beds!" cries the landlady, dismantling the stretcher frames and spitting on the canvases, at the bottom of which the artist has scrawled his name: Modigliani. The year is 1915. As the war rages outside, Fujita spends all day painting. When he becomes too hungry to paint, he goes to the butcher's and asks if there's any leftover liver. He says it's for his cat, but the cat is him.

One October, Alexia left for Barcelona. "Spain's a hundred years behind the rest of the world!" I said when she showed me a landscape painting she had bought there.

"Almodóvar's behind?" she said. "Felipe González is behind?"

Never having had her finger on the political pulse, she nonetheless had made herself scarce just two months before the December 2001 riots. She rang me not long after her departure and, gabbling as ever, asked if I wanted the good news or the *really* good news. The good was that she'd made a contact in Catalan TV. And the really good? She was seeing an older man, a forty-four-year-old who drove a red Ferrari, went around in white jeans, and owned hotels in Mauritius. "I know, I know," she said, "it's only temporary, though. What's that noise? Is that the protests? Go over to a window, will you, let me listen for a minute." They had already begun to sound like a foreign language to her, the drumbeat of an indigenous tribe she could no longer decipher.

Her Catalan TV contact turned out to be no help at all, but, not to be dissuaded, she began sending her CV to *La Vanguardia*, with ideas for articles enclosed: "Who Rules Among the Squatters?"; "Fear and Loathing in Park Güell." She never received any replies. Spain had more than its fair share of Latin Americans trying to make new lives for themselves, and the newspaper mailbags were overflowing with suggestions from would-be neo-gonzo journalists. Her Ferrari lover went away to London and didn't give a return date. Showing all his experience, he left her the keys to his apartment and waited two weeks before calling to say she could drop them at his office after she had moved out. She threw them in the nearest sewer and got a temp job in a department store. It was December and they put her in the Christmas section. She had always been a dab hand at curling ribbon with a pair of scissors, but, as it turned out, Spanish women prefer their ribbons uncurled. "They see it as some kind of Argentinian affectation," she said. "Everything's so basic here!"

One day she rang and announced she'd signed up to do a professional development course for journalists, a monthlong primer in international economics. This was someone who couldn't even make sense of her own bank statements. At the end of the course, ten of the students were going to be selected to form a team of reporters who would then be sent on assignments around the world. The company running the course was called SinergiC InternationaL—the four capital letters didn't do a great deal, in my eyes, for its legitimacy. I looked it up online, but it didn't even have a website. She made the top ten in the exam; she was in. Her first assignment was in Africa.

"Angola," she said on the phone. "Just imagine the killer novel I'm going to write after all this."

Fujita has left a wife behind in Japan, but she rarely enters his thoughts. Traveling alone is less unwieldy; you can be lighter on your feet. And if you create a character for yourself, people will start noticing you. So it is that Fujita soon becomes Foujita. The pictures the Parisians buy—or wrest from him the moment the paint is dry—go hand in hand with the personality. Foujita pulls up at Café le Dôme every day in a little Ballot sports car, a bronze Rodin sculpture as the hood mascot. He slips from the automobile into the awaiting crowd. People have climbed trees to get a better view. Stopping at the door of the café, he turns and bows, saying a few words in Japanese. Nobody understands, but nobody admits it either: yellow fever has taken over the country. Everybody wants a piece of Foujita, even if only the tiniest enchanting whiff. His round spectacles, the gold earrings, the fringe like an upside-down bowl of rice, and that finest of mustaches, seemingly done in charcoal. "Which character from history would you like to have been?" calls out a journalist from his position halfway up a lamppost. "Adam," he answers: "The first ever European."

The idea of the collective, so fundamental to the Japanese spirit, is enough to bring him out in hives. Instead of the fish, temples, and cherry trees of his peers at home, Foujita takes languid women as his subject, mixing his ink stick with oil paint. All of the School of Paris applauds his work. Most intriguing to them is his use of white, a white never seen before, a new band in the rainbow that comes from mixing talc, white lead, and calcium in proportions known only to the artist's cat, who is the sole witness to the mixing process.

Foujita also produces a number of self-portraits at this

time—accompanied by that crafty-looking cat. He never gives the creature a name, but his friends call it Fou-Fou. He says he paints cats to give his eyes a rest. But if you look at these portraits, everything that Foujita's own figure withholds can be discerned in that of the cat: the nervousness, the anxieties, the hunger for recognition. The one held in the Buenos Aires National Museum of Fine Arts is a case in point. He bequeathed it after a 1932 exhibition of his work there that helped to forge his legend: more than 60,000 visitors came, and at one point Foujita had to hide in the storage rooms when the hordes of waiting fans got out of hand.

In Alexia's first months away I asked her to send me any writing she was doing. "Sure," she'd always say, "as soon as we get off the phone," before promptly forgetting all about it. Every now and then I'd get a photo as an e-mail attachment, but this was just as impersonal as being sent a postcard. When she told me about the places she'd been visiting, it felt little more than a guided tour with headphones. I'd hear all about the months she spent living in five-star hotels, but never the names of the people she was working with. There was sometimes talk of promotions, but the hierarchy in the company made no sense to me at all: one day she was a journalist and another an interpreter, consultant, or location scout. I couldn't help but wonder what she was really doing. I began imagining outlandish scenes, and these grew more rarefied the vaguer she was. Had she become a spy? No way, too much of a loudmouth. A high-priced escort? Too obvious. Was she involved in some awful scheme selling Bangladeshi babies? No, she wasn't coldhearted enough. Finding no answers, I started going the other way: Had she possibly just taken a job writing tawdry advertorials?

She once told me she had interviewed three economics ministers at an African political summit.

"What, so corruption incarnate?" I said.

"No, not at all. Interesting people," she said, her newfound political correctness so improbable I wondered if someone was tapping the phone.

I would have slapped her if we'd been in the same place. She still wasn't anywhere near being the journalist or superstar writer she had set out to be, and wouldn't admit it. She was only keeping up this sham career as a nod to our friendship. She felt so far away that I started to call her Angola.

Once a year, on her annual visit to Buenos Aires, Angola would call to arrange a lunch date. She always chose the most expensive places, and always arrived late, a waft of new perfume accompanying her entrance every time. Her hair was short—*très* European—and her natural wheaty blond now came out of a bottle. Lots of annoying Spanish idioms had entered her speech, and when she began to opine on Argentina she screwed up her mouth. She always insisted on paying, whipping out a company credit card to do so. But we still managed to reduce each other to fits of laughter—"Laughing like we're going to kill ourselves," as she put it—and I would end up dabbing my face with the napkin, begging her to stop because my cheeks were hurting.

I don't know, though, that we still had the ability to read each other. It was like we thought we knew each other so well that we'd stopped being able to see each other with any clarity. I felt that Alexia, the golden girl of my youth, had dried up, grown brittle, somewhere along the way. And what might she have thought of me? That much was obvious: still the same stick-in-the-mud as always, still *a total drag.*

In 1933, Foujita cuts his moorings once more. He goes back to Japan, and the "o" goes from his name. "When I sit on the tatami and dip my brush, all those years I spent away become a distant memory," he tells a Tokyo newspaper. When Japan invades China, it prompts the worst kitsch of his entire career: the government tasks him with commemorating the hostilities, and he is only too happy to oblige, coming up with a hundred images of pure bellicose silliness. *Final Fighting in Attu*, from 1942, is an unfeeling junk shop of dismembered bodies. Astonishing that the same artist was responsible for the marmoreal sensuality of *Reclining Nude with Toile de Jouy* twenty years before. The eccentric flâneur who once strolled arm in arm with Isadora Duncan, toga and all, is now to be seen in army fatigues, and stands in a salute as members of the public file past his works, next to which there is a donation box for the war effort.

But personal glory has always been his real goal, since day one. When the United States enters the fray, eventually pulverizing Japan, off comes the military garb: he offers himself to General MacArthur as a maker of Christmas cards. Over time his chameleonic personality and his love of the spotlight dissolve his talent: the more he moves away from himself, the less interesting his work becomes. It is as though his first act of betrayal has sparked a compulsive chain of further betrayals, and Fujita gradually loses sight of who he really is. He returns to France in the 1950s, buys an eighteenth-century château, and changes his name to Léonard (in honor of Leonardo da Vinci). He dons one final mask when, feeling death draw near, he converts to Catholicism: he designs his own outfit and sends out invitations to the ceremony in Reims Cathedral. But, except for a couple of children who hide in one of the confessionals shouting "Fou! Fou!" throughout the service, nobody comes.

I was taken to an ophthalmologist as a child, having been complaining of seeing double. Diplopia, they called the affliction. As a corrective, I was made to peer through some optical apparatus at a pair of Sylvester the Cats up on the wall; they were separated by a white space, and I had to use my eye muscles to bring them together, pulling them both into the middle so that one lay on top of the other. Looking at Angola across the restaurant table, during my annual visitation, was like seeing two obdurately discrete silhouettes: there was no way of bringing them together, no way of forcing one to lie atop the other.

"Still writing poetry?" she asked me the last time I saw her. "Gothic, despairing, all that?"

"I am."

"And are you thinking of doing anything with it?"

"I'm not sure. I need to write more, I just struggle to find gaps."

"Flake," she said, seeming to summarize two decades' worth of unspoken sentiment. "Writing doesn't happen in gaps."

Who the hell are you? I felt like saying. *Who* are *you?* And though I immediately felt horrible for even thinking this, I was tired of her secrets, and of the way she had always kept me at arm's length in her personal quest for—what to call it? Success? Self-realization? When, on autopilot, I suggested we try to meet up again before she left, she said she had a lot to do but, yes, she'd try to find a "gap" (doing scare quotes with her fingers). She'd call me. She asked for the bill, paid, and I went out with her to hail a taxi. We hugged, briefly, insubstantially. Before the taxi pulled away, she wound down the window:

"Shall I send you my novel when it's done?"

"You'd better," I said, and I wanted to say something else, something truthful, but the lights turned green and I only had time to add: "But watch out for your scarf, or you'll come to the same end as Isadora."

When what I really wanted to say was: "Didn't you go too far?"

In my mind there is a door with a sign on it: "Do Not Disturb: Crisis Underway." Chet Baker's "You Can't Go Home Again" drifts out, along with the smell of mentholated Virginia Slims. There, take a glass, put your ear to the door, and you'll hear it: two girls whispering and giggling all night long. This is the room where she lives, my brilliant, beautiful friend, the one I've lost. A part of me lives in there with her—a big part of me. To this day, every time I come home I check the post, hoping my hand will alight on the parcel containing her novel. Sometimes, on the rare, brief occasion when I manage to put my infinite insecurities aside, I hope with all my soul that what I find will be enormous, a 400-page tome, and that with it my misgivings, all the questioning, will finally come to an end.

LIGHTNING AT SEA

The first time I went to Mar del Plata was in winter. My boyfriend and I and a couple of friends traveled down in a borrowed Ford pickup. We went for the surf, or they did; I would have loved to go in too but I was also scared. It was my job to guard the Ford, making sure no one stole the bags or the sound system. Parked a few meters back from the cliff top, a Doors cassette playing over and over, I sat rolling spliffs as skinny as pine needles and reading *I Visited Ganymede*, a copy of which I'd found in the glove box. And gazing out at the boys. In their black neoprene, through the constant sea mist, they looked like wolves of the water. I don't know how I put up with such expanses of dead time; maybe it was being a teenager and therefore living outside of time, or in a kind of time that just didn't correspond somehow. My only problem, the one thing I concerned myself with in those days, was fitting in. Everything in life felt like the boots of German World War I soldiers, who weren't given left and right, but rather two shaped exactly the same. Go on, then, get on with it. I think this was why I didn't mind the waiting. Sitting looking out to sea, smoking endless spliffs, I engaged in a more private kind of surfing, conducted entirely in the confines of my mind.

I know of no one who has wanted to be a writer and failed to dedicate at least a few lines to the sea. The ones that have always stuck with me, for some reason, are by women. Marguerite Duras: "Since I came to the sea, I have known nothing." Marina Tsvetaeva: "I do not love the sea, the sea has no counterpoint." Sylvia Plath: "It drags the sea after it like a dark crime." I added my quota when I was younger, in a series of unforgivable sonnets, and will do so again now—but not in verse. (Fear not.) I will just say one or two things; a personal history of this body of water, perhaps.

The first stage in my infatuation came as a teenager: I fell for a seascape by Courbet that I saw in a documentary at school. When I found out that one of his works was held in a gallery near to where I lived, no more than a bus ride away, I went to see it and the fixation only intensified. It was at the National Museum of Fine Arts, and the piece was *The Stormy Sea*, *Mer orageuse* in French, the rasping consonants replicating the roar of the waves. A foamy roller breaks against rocks in the foreground; at the horizon, the sea and sky meld into one; and in the top half of the picture the sky is packed with bulging pinkish clouds. This oil on canvas from 1869 is close to one meter high and one meter wide, just right to hang on my chimney breast, if I had one. How lovely it would be to watch a fire burning beneath such a sea! Every time I look at it, something inside me becomes compressed, a sensation between my chest and my throat, like a small bite being taken out of me. I have learned to respect this twinge, to pay attention to it, because my body always works things out before I do. Only afterward does my intellect draw its conclusions.

Courbet was a territorial painter, and instinctive as a dog. He grew up on the French side of the Jura Mountains, where the rains funnel down through cracks in the limestone, down cliffs, caves, and valleys, to form underground channels. Courbet transferred the textures of this landscape to the seas he painted. He was a devil with the palette knife: scraping and gouging at the canvas as though etching on rock. For all his tough-guy posturing, and all the tactics he employed to gain notoriety, there was this endless return to the region of his childhood. His water was fossil-like: a slab of malachite rent hard across the middle. What is it about this picture that has always attracted me? Some minerals, when placed under UV lights, stay lit up for several days afterward. "Phosphorescence" is the term given to this period of sustained luminosity. Courbet's sea was like that, a bright nodule in my mind for days.

When Courbet was twenty he went to Paris for a prolonged immersion in all that the Louvre had to offer. He studied Titian, Francisco de Zurbarán, Rembrandt, and Rubens. He took on certain of their techniques, while leaving aside the traditional values in whose name these painters had employed them. Courbet couldn't have been less interested in ideas of purity; all he wanted was to create pictures to saturate the senses. Hence Peter Schjeldahl's line about seeing a Courbet and being gripped by the urge to go running off down the streets, to incite the people, to have sex, or to eat an apple. The viewer is sent into a pictorial fever.

The Salon, the annual or biennial art exhibition of the Académie des Beaux-Arts in Paris, acted as a filter for countless works of art. The walls would be crammed with pictures; what could an artist do to catch the public's eye? It was at this time that Courbet discovered newspapers. He was the first painter to realize that controversy might not damage your profile: a bad reputation could be good publicity. He'd make friends with anyone if he saw some advantage in it, including Proudhon, Berlioz, and Baudelaire, none of whom were that moved by his work, though they couldn't help but respect his tenacity. In the years leading up to the 1848 Revolution, Courbet helped establish Realism, a movement second only in importance to Romanticism, though far more nebulous.

He turned his eye to beggars, vagabonds, washerwomen, and miners. His ragged country peasants were part of an honest attempt to render the truths of the world. But it wasn't so much his themes as his methods that attracted criticism: when his subject was a stone breaker, he turned him into an object as crude as the stone he was breaking. And the same with the sea. The acute level of observation he brought to bear on his landscapes, combined with the rough energy of his brush, not only reaches back to forebears like Turner, and to the Dutch painters of the eighteenth century, but anticipates everything to come in painting from 1870 onward. *The Stormy Sea*, while clinging fast to the line of the horizon, comprises a formal interrogation of water, thereby leading directly on to the work of later abstract artists.

At one time there was no body of water between the cliffs of Dover and the porous and equally white coast of Normandy—the Alabaster Coast, as it is known in France. An area on the French side, in Pays de Caux, has long been a pilgrimage site for artists. It was here, on the chalk cliffs around the town of Étretat, that the sea captivated Courbet, circa 1869. Sailors in the area dubbed him the Seal, for the long hours he spent motionless on the rocks, studying their shapes and colors. It was here that he painted his first seascapes.

Guy de Maupassant passed through Étretat that same year, and came across the painter, going on to describe the encounter in the Paris periodical *Gil Blas*:

> In a huge, empty room, a fat, dirty, greasy man was slapping white paint on a blank canvas with a kitchen knife. From time to time he would press his face against the window and look out at the storm. The sea came so close that it seemed to batter the house and completely envelop it in its foam and roar. The salty water beat against the windowpanes like hail, and ran down the walls. On his mantelpiece was a bottle of cider next to a half-filled glass. Now and then, Courbet would take

> a few swigs, and then return to his work. This work became *The Stormy Sea*, and caused quite a sensation around the world.

The critics didn't know how to react, but other painters were in no doubt. Manet called Courbet the king of the sea. His treatment of light and water was largely stolen from Eugène Boudin—the king of the sky—who must have realized that he had erred in his choice of subject: the sea always sold far better than the sky. The latter never transfers very gracefully onto canvas, coming out either mellifluous or inert. Whereas the sea . . . you always get good returns on the sea. The next time you go on a seaside vacation and there's a rainy day, visit any local art gallery and you'll see for yourself.

There are some thirty-five Courbet paintings of calm seas, and another thirty of squalls, but in Buenos Aires I have only ever seen two, and they are both in the National Museum of Fine Arts. Those I've seen in other forms—on the internet and in library books—are all surpassed by *The Stormy Sea*. When you stand before it, art disappears and something else rushes in: life, in all its tempestuousness. I would bet that Courbet himself, who used to boast of dashing off his seascapes in two hours flat, would have been proud of this one. He returned to it time and again, like a thirsty horse to its trough.

There was something about water that made him forget the grand gestures, cleaving his public aspect from his private. To the outside world he was the loudmouth who proclaimed himself the only painter of the century, and all the rest either his disciples or idiots; the braggart who responded to his noninclusion in the 1855 World's Fair by setting up his own pavilion; the man who, during the uprisings of the Paris Commune, coolly joined the crowd that toppled the Napoleonic column in Place Vendôme. But he was not bereft of an inner life, this painter of stormy seas, this troubled soul for whom water was the only salve. He later went into exile in Switzerland after fleeing the French authorities, quickly grew tired of quaint tourist commissions, and drank himself into an early grave at the age of fifty-eight. He died on New Year's Eve 1877, a week after his Paris home and all his worldly belongings had been put up for public auction.

I do not see *The Stormy Sea* as a symbolic painting, or a tragic meditation on life. It is Courbet's way of submitting to the order of things, in the same way Marcus Aurelius did when he came to the Hron River in AD 178, saying: "Let the universe decide."

There is a film I come across occasionally when watching late-night TV that never fails to hypnotize me. It's about a group of American surfers who rob banks wearing ex-president masks. These are surfers with a cause, spiritual gangsters who read the Old Testament and proclaim the coming of Jesus. (Now that I think about it, Jesus was the first ever surfer, the first to walk on water . . .) The police set out to infiltrate the group, and though the officer they appoint finds himself seduced by its mystique, all is going according to plan until some girl trouble moves us swiftly on to the denouement. In the final scene, the officer confronts the leader of the surfer bank robbers, a messiah figure obsessed with catching *the* wave, the one that appears as the result of a hundred-year swell in the oceans. On the day of the storm we see the two of them on a beach in Australia: the police officer has followed him there, I think rain is falling, and beyond them in the distance the water begins to rear up. The officer gets handcuffs on the surfer king, who begs him to take them off—to be allowed to go out into the water. The officer knows that he'll be sending him to his death, but it is a death that at least accords with his beliefs. As they argue, rain beating down, the water continues to surge forward. The waves, thick as milk, or cream, or stew, are straight out of a Courbet.

The sun was going down, lighting the funereal clouds blood-purple. I got out of the pickup and began making signals, waving my arms. The boys exited the water one by one, measured, stately, like wandering monks, and on the drive home we stopped off at the Boston Café for croissants, some of the best croissants I've eaten in my life. The house we were staying in had belonged to my grandparents and now lay empty because of an inheritance dispute between my mother and her siblings. Persuading my parents to let us go had been a feat in itself: my mother hated my boyfriend, still held hopes of me marrying a polo player someday (a glimpse of my mother the negotiator: she liked money, I liked horses: voila), and furthermore didn't think it was right for a teenage girl to travel without a chaperone of some kind. But eventually I ground her down. And we went off for a weekend in that old stone house, its shell solid as anything, but everything inside touched by the threat of collapse: the wooden stairs rotten, the corners dotted with little pyramids of sawdust from the termites, and wind rattling through the tired bedrooms. In the sprawling master bedroom my boyfriend and I had sex to keep warm. Footsteps went up and down outside: the house also had a walker of hallways at night. This was a cousin of mine, a girl, or young woman really, five years older than me, who had fled Buenos Aires a few months earlier. When no one came to drag her home (I suspect they found her easier to deal with at arm's length), she stayed on. We hardly spoke, but she had the most beautiful smile, and when we coincided for breakfast she would show me how to make bracelets with Rastafarian-colored beads. My fingers, like hers, were long and spidery—a family trait—and I picked it up quickly. I think she didn't mind our presence because we took care not to upset her routine. Her single pastime was cutting up old magazines to make collages, always in blue and green. Those were the only colors she would use. The week we showed up, she had begun covering the walls of her room. The plan, she said, was to cover everything, ceiling included.

My cousin was also drawn to the sea. She would get in the water religiously, regardless of the color of the lifeguards' flag. If it was cold, she just put a wetsuit on. We watched from the terrace and placed bets on how long it would take her to give up and come back in. But even if it was raining—even if pouring—she'd go on swimming a little longer, as though she knew all about our bets, as though mocking the city dwellers we were, ridiculing our fear of a sudden lightning strike out across the water. My cousin was eccentric, and I liked that: it made me proud to see someone bucking family convention. We never talked about her reasons for leaving Buenos Aires, but I knew why she'd left, I sensed it. We had the same blood, after all. Only once did I let slip that I'd heard her walking around at night. Blushing, she then said, like someone shooing a fly:

"I don't know what it is I go looking for."

She stayed on in Mar del Plata, and had a child three years later with a local guy who promptly made himself scarce. The last time I went down there (with a new man in tow, still not the polo player of my mother's dreams) she was quite changed: her son was not yet a year old, and on our arrival she took him and departed to some distant corner of the house. She didn't come down for breakfasts, and she no longer swam in the sea.

But her night walking went on. She patrolled the hallways like a soul in torment, and left the baby to cry and cry, wherever it was. I remember peeking out through the half-open door and not knowing what to do. When you are in the vicinity of someone on the edge of madness, a moment comes, a very clear moment, in which your watching tips over into voyeurism. That last night I saw the lightning flash inside her mind. I have never told anyone about what I saw. I wouldn't know who to tell.

She and I spoke just once during that stay, on the afternoon of our departure. She took me up to her room and showed me the collage-covered walls. It was like seeing one of Courbet's waves from the inside.

"Nearly done." She smiled—a little too much, like a person with nothing left to lose.

Some months later I found out that she had hanged herself. Not far from the jetty on the north side of the beach, on an afternoon of blue skies—just a handful of pinkish clouds hovering. The house soon sold to a hotel chain, and I was sent to Mar del Plata to sign some paperwork. Although the renovation was already underway, I took the chance to go in one final time. I walked around the garden, the only place not crawling with construction workers. And suddenly felt a tug like a fishing line reeling me in. I went and asked if I could go upstairs, and made my way to her room: I wanted to see the collages, I had an urge to take at least one of them with me, but when I went in, the walls were bare, or blank: expanses of nothing but flat white paint. I hunted through all the wardrobes in the house, I asked some workers who were putting up a glass screen on the sea terrace, but they didn't know what I was talking about. I insisted: they had to be somewhere. I never found them.

My cousin was also called María. And only recently has it come to me that our name has the sea in it—*mar*—embedded like a lure, like a foretelling.

OUT OF THE TRAPS

At my friend Amalia's the other night, while she cooked us supper, I took a look at her bookshelves. I tried to act natural, but I was surveying them like a pickpocket. Quick, furtive glances. I knew how improper this was really, how akin to going through another person's medicine cabinet. Both are activities I find impossible to resist, for the revelations they promise. It was as I examined the broken spines, specifically the region stretching from Nabokov to Pushkin, on the shelf right in front of *Look at the Harlequins!*, that I noticed a small bronze ball on a block of red silk. It stood out because Amalia doesn't have decorative objects in her apartment—none. She belongs to Those Who Live

Light, a scattered race of people who go through life doing anything they can to avoid amassing junk. No silver plinths in the bathroom here, no porcelain Buddha figures cluttering the kitchen countertops, no African masks on the walls. I don't know if Amalia's monkish austerity is genetic, or rather what another friend has identified as a late symptom of her self-enforced downward mobility. She has adhered to the ethics of renunciation for years, a discipline aimed not at descending the social ladder precisely but certainly at shunning any kind of rise. In all the time I had known Amalia, I'd never seen anything in her Paternal studio apartment that could even remotely be described as decorative. So why this bronze ball? I immediately wanted one as well and, unable to help myself, I asked her, with barely veiled covetousness, where she got it. "It was a present," she said, and I noticed a flicker in her eyes. "It's a dorodango."

One morning, Amalia got a phone call. A woman at the other end of the line said she was looking for someone to teach her Spanish. She was Japanese, and had recently arrived in Argentina. She needed to practice conversation: she had the basics, but wanted to become more fluent. Amalia's parents are Japanese, and she was working as an in-house translator at a publishing firm at the time.

It had been a while since she'd given Spanish classes to compatriots of her parents, but something in the woman's voice—which was calm, and gravelly but also honeyed—intrigued her. They agreed to meet the following day. The woman had an apartment on Avenida Libertador, and when Amalia described the entrance, I knew exactly which building it was. She took the elevator up to the twenty-first floor and, unaccustomed to heights, lost her stomach slightly when she stepped out. The woman let her in, a chill elegance to her demeanor. Her dark hair scraped back into a bun, and her skin taut, she was stunningly, alarmingly beautiful, like a character out of a spy movie. She led Amalia through into a bright room: floor-to-ceiling windows, white walls, low armchairs, and a dotting of chrome lamps. Amalia, her momentary queasiness past, went over to the window. The apartment overlooked the Hippodrome and, there being no balcony, she found nothing but thin air between her and the rings in the sand all that way below.

"Horses, I say to the estate agents. We want a view of *horses*."

Amalia took a few deep breaths to find her balance and, once she felt the ground regain solidity beneath her feet, turned around. A girl was standing in the doorway on the far side of the room, fifteen or so, skinny arms, blue sweater. Her straight, shoulder-length hair was the lustrous black of a crow's feathers in the rain. She smiled, the darkness of her pupils apparently bottomless. When she approached, Amalia noticed that she dragged her right foot. Her name was Miuki and she had been born with one leg three centimeters shorter than the other, hence the platform shoe and her gait. She would be taking part in the classes.

The mother mentioned that Miuki's father was a Nissan executive, recently transferred to work in the Argentinian arm of the business. (It was the 1980s, and every other car on the road was Japanese.) The two of them had been sent ahead to begin settling in, and to kit out the apartment.

For the next few months, between five and six every Thursday afternoon, Amalia conversed in Spanish with her two students. Language learning: serious conversations about the most trivial subjects. The daughter made quick progress, the mother did not. They sat at a round glass table next to the window—floating, it felt like, off to one side of the Hippodrome racetrack. The starting gun could not be heard at that distance, but when the traps flew open and the horses burst forward, the students started in their seats.

Amalia never saw the husband. Over time, she began to think that mother and daughter were the same person, split in two. They were uncannily alike in appearance and in the way they spoke, though the girl's features had yet to harden like those of her mother. December came, and as they were gathering up the exercise books at the end of a class, the mother announced that this would be the last. She apologized for the abruptness of it, but they had been called back to Japan. Amalia was at a loss; she had started looking forward to these classes, they'd become a high point in her week. She wanted to understand, but they looked back at her as if already very far away, as if themselves part of a distant landscape. In the elevator, just as the doors were about to shut, Miuki handed her a small package, wrapped elegantly in red cloth. Inside was the dorodango. Amalia had heard of them but never before held one.

Since time immemorial, children in Kyoto have been taught to work mud with their hands; sitting together in circles, they take a clump and roll it until it is the size and shape of a billiard ball. They work for hours in the sun, leave the balls to dry in the shade, dip them in water, and go on working, however long it takes. Over time the balls of mud transform into polished bronze spheres. Work on the dorodango only a little too much, and cracks appear. The technique is passed down over generations; only the most tenacious master it.

•

I know the apartment building Amalia described because I used to pass it every day as a child when I took the dog for walks. They were long walks: my way of unspooling the parental fishing line lodged in my twelve-year-old cheek. "Someone has to take this dog out!" I'd scream, in one of my perennial furies. The dachshund, unperturbed—tail wagging—followed me to the elevator. One day the walk went on too long, and my parents called the police. A couple of officers were standing outside the entrance to our building when I did finally get back. Neither said a word, but it was clear from the looks on their faces that I was the problem. I avoided any confrontation by going in through the servants' entrance, my avoidance tactic of choice. After that I made sure to leave a note saying I'd taken the dog out, thereby guaranteeing myself two hours' freedom a day.

The first time we made it as far as the Hippodrome, it was a race day. At that time the track had an encircling wall, meaning it was impossible to see in from the street, but at one point the upper portion of the wall gave way to an iron grille. The perfect spyhole. I was a good climber, and needed no invitation; up I went, dachshund looking on forlornly. From this vantage the track opened out before me in wide sand ellipses; beyond, the interlocking paddocks and grandstands shimmered in the sun. I saw the horses, jockeys mounted, pacing before entering the traps. Minutes later, the air began to prickle like the prelude to a summer storm, and then it happened: the reverberating crack of the starting gun, the traps clattering open, a prickling bloom in my chest, and those bright streaks in the distance: they raced past me, their hewn, glossy forms lathered in sweat; a thundering glimpse of pure distilled animal will.

The problem was the days when there were no races.

I got to my grille-peephole one day and, finding the tracks deserted, decided to just carry on walking. Half an hour later, swerving between nannies and their strollers, pausing periodically for the dachshund to catch breath, I came to a building with a faded pink facade. I was aware that it was an art museum although, unusually, I had never been inside. Unusually because of Mama's mania for the visual arts. Every time we went to New York, more or less as soon as we arrived, my brother and I would be dragged along to the Met. She was obsessed. We'd get out of the taxi, and the two of us would have to run so as not to lose her among all those papyruses, sarcophagi, and mummies. When she finally reached her destination, Monet's water lilies, she would let out a sigh, and only then could we sit and digest the scrambled eggs she had made us wolf down at the hotel.

Though I am now able to appreciate Monet's "lovely style," he has never moved me. I've never been able to dive into his work in any serious way. My mother put this down to my brittle nerves. In fact it is something else entirely, only I didn't have the words to formulate it in those days. It is my view that any artist too dependent on either seeking or presenting new and astonishing experiences will cease to be effective once he or she succeeds in, as it were, apportioning that sense of discovery. By restricting his art to a solely visual sensation, I think Monet was merely scratching a surface. Anyway, I was more taken with the infant mummy in its ash-colored bandages, glimpsed on our dash through the Egyptian room. Carson McCullers said it better: "You mean right here in the corner of your eye. (*She points to her eye.*) You suddenly catch something there. And this cold shiver runs all the way down you."

No one had ever said anything about the pink museum twenty blocks from my house. I later found out that, to my parents, the Buenos Aires of my childhood held no artistic interest; they spent their lives paralyzed by a kind of neurotic torpor generated by seeing themselves reflected in the past, in all the city mansions, in every bronze statue and every silver dinner service, theirs or anyone else's. That afternoon, a group of teenage boys had gathered on the steps outside the building, and as I passed them with my dog a gust of wind hit me head-on, too suddenly for me to do anything about my plaid school skirt flying up. The boys burst out laughing. I gave them my best death stare, such a thing in those days as could shatter glass, but when the doors to the museum opened I tied up the dog and trailed in after them. I wandered around, looking at this and that, unsure of where a person was supposed to stand. The place was full of the boys' whispers, and every now and then I'd run into them again.

Then I saw it: the size of an office folder, it was called *En observation—M. Fabre, Officier de reserve* and it was by someone called Henri de Toulouse-Lautrec. What was it about this picture? There were horses in it. Even now, that is what strikes me first, and the first thing that then drops away. There were other things in it, a lot of green, for example, the infamous Toulouse-Lautrec green, although I wouldn't find that out until a decade later at school. An army officer stands with his back to us, scanning the horizon with a pair of binoculars. Behind him, another soldier, on horseback, holds the reins of his horse. The riderless horse is the only one looking at us, and its hind legs are bent, seemingly about to kick out. About to wake us, that is, from the self-indulgent somnolence in which Impressionism has mired us. But I didn't know that then either.

It is hard to imagine a more privileged environment than that of the Hôtel du Bosc palace in Albi, where Toulouse-Lautrec was born. He came from a family of aristocratic reactionaries that claimed an unbroken lineage back to Louis VI, and his father, Alphonse Charles Comte de Toulouse-Lautrec-Monfa, was an eccentric who went around in chain mail and thought more highly of horses than he did of people. He would ride into the village in summer with his falcon on his shoulder, feeding it strips of raw meat and dispensing little sips of holy water from a bottle—so as not to deprive the bird of the benefits of a spiritual life.

The family coursed, overflowed, with vital energy. In the eighteenth century, Adelaide de Toulouse had boasted that no man existed, "neither servant nor lord, city-dweller nor country mouse," with whom she had not shared a bed. Such hedonists were the Toulouses, and so simultaneously opposed to the idea of outsiders getting hands on their fortune, that they began intermarrying. Henri, the result of the marriage between Alphonse and his first cousin Adèle, was born with an unknown genetic disorder, possibly pycnodysostosis; his bones were extremely brittle, and his torso developed to adult size while his legs remained those of a child. At the age of twelve he fell from a chair and broke his left femur, and then the right in another minor fall soon after. In his mid-teens he was four feet nine and, despite all the attentions he received, he would grow less than another inch over the course of the rest of his life.

"We Toulouses get in the saddle the moment we are

born," said Count Alphonse. "But not my son." The leg breaks meant he had to spend his time in the dullest pastime ever invented: the seeing of doctors. He spent his days on the terrace that overlooked the palace grounds, sprawled on a lawn chair, his world restricted to a view of the walnut trees above and of the army of physicians that buzzed around him. All he wanted in the world was to straddle a horse, but he found himself condemned to the sidelines. And so he began painting them. "Nothing in the world electrifies me so," he told his father, running his paintbrush over the nostrils of a sorrel mare as it dipped its head for him. The count, as though picking up the thread of a long-ago conversation, replied: "Remember, my boy, that the healthy life can only be lived out-of-doors. Anything that is not free will deform, and eventually die."

The aristocratic ambience felt like death to Henri. The one person with whom he developed a rapport was René Princeteau, a deaf-mute painter who showed him the basics of technique and encouraged him to go to Paris. Like any class deserter, he was welcomed like a son in Montmartre. The prince of the Albi forest found in the women he encountered there—with all their grace and incredible brio—substitutes for his horses. He was so short that it made the prostitutes dizzy to look down at him, but the little man had the ability to identify secret zones on their bodies, places just as smooth as lips. When he looked in the mirror Lautrec was presented with the protuberance of his nose, the pince-nez, his big puffy lips, the little bow-legs. His physical eccentricities extended to his alarming genitalia: in the brothels he earned the nicknames "Tri-pod" and "Coffee Pot." He walked with a stick, which he also used to poke around between the girls' legs; how he loved to ruffle those skirts. The Social Hygiene Brigade came and checked on the cabaret in the evenings, and only after they departed would the girls relax, feet going straight up on the tables, calves stretched out like small stone balustrades, and tossing into the air their frothy pet-ticoats, their silk scarves, their ribbons and lace.

Lautrec kept a table reserved at the Moulin Rouge, and on the wall behind it he showed his work. Away from his roots, life was harder, but he could at least breathe. One of his drinking companions picked up a pencil from the ta-ble once and, handing it to him, said: "Sir, you forgot your stick." One of the dancers, on seeing a lithograph: "You, sir, have a flair for deformities." "So I've always been told," he replied. "Since the moment I was born." He befriended these women, these profane fin de siècle Madonnas, and his posters ensured their immortality. They complained that he made them ugly, yet all carried on modeling for him. Redheads were his favorite; "God's blondes," he called them. Popó, La Rouge, and Mademoiselle Carotte played dice, bathed together, lounged on divans like cats in heat, their guard down completely as the half-man sat sketching away, all the while drinking, drinking—small but constant, unending sips. His mustache was never dry.

His economical style absorbed aspects of contemporary Japanese art—the art of the Ukiyo, or Floating World, period: the more sordid, the better; the more sensual, intelligent, and perverse, the better. Blocks of black, oblique angles, the sinuous lines of the figures. Lautrec was an artist of the floating Parisian world, and the brothel and cabaret were as crucial to his work as the teahouses were to Utamaro's. He dreamed of visiting Japan, but could find no one willing to go with him. He had heard that the men in those faraway islands, which had recently opened their doors to the world, were the same height as him.

Twenty years after her students' sudden departure, Amalia visited Tokyo. When she got up to her hotel room, she took out an old Filofax and dialed a number. Miuki answered and said she was pleased to hear from Amalia, though her voice was subdued. She had no plans that evening and agreed to meet in a bar in Shinjuku. Amalia arrived late after struggling to find a taxi, and it then took her some time to locate Miuki; the bar was deafeningly loud and mirrored pillars created a confusion of duplicated red-felt tablecloths, waiters, and bottles of whiskey.

Finally she spotted her at the bar. Going over, first pawing the air in front of her face to check it wasn't another trick of the eye, she found a woman well into her thirties, her allure faded; wrinkles fanned out at the corners of her eyes when she looked up, smiling. A walking stick with a tortoiseshell handle was resting against the adjacent stool. Miuki ordered them two beers and proceeded to talk nonstop, in surprisingly good Spanish.

Her mother was orphaned in World War II and then raised in a Catholic convent, she told Amalia. Her good looks and natural reserve had opened the door to a good marriage: in aspirational 1960s Japan, Catholic convents were considered a reliable source of decent wives. Her husband, however, was only interested in business. And when Miuki was born physically defective, he distanced himself even more. In fact, the Buenos Aires episode was a good illustration of how the marriage functioned: mother and daughter would be sent ahead somewhere to prepare the way, but in the interim the father would be given a different posting, and the women called back with no explanations.

Miuki's mother died in a freak car accident soon after the return from Buenos Aires, and Miuki won a place at university to study history. She found the new environment difficult to adapt to. Her mother had dedicated herself totally to Miuki's upbringing; all her life had been about polishing her, in some attempt to help her avoid experiencing pain. The result was the temperament of a delicate hothouse flower, and when her university peers refused to make exceptions for her, she found life extremely difficult to navigate. She fainted on the library steps one day, and a passing medical student came to her aid. He graduated shortly after, and a year later they were married. She gave up her studies to accompany him to the town of Matsumoto, where he had found work in the municipal hospital. Two years later they divorced. Miuki's exquisite manners became a source of vexation for her husband. She was so much more refined than his colleagues' wives, who never accepted her as one of them. "They polished you too much, Miuki," he'd say during their fights. "They spoiled you."

Miuki went back to Tokyo. Her father suffered from diabetes, and had gone blind; he needed someone at his side. "What else was I going to do?" she said to Amalia in the bar. "A woman my age, a divorcée, no children. I'm like a still life, no good to anyone." Her gaze had grown distant. At that moment it occurred to Amalia, who had always carried the dorodango in her purse like a talisman, to give it back, but, worried at giving offense, she decided against the idea.

•

At the age of thirty, Lautrec looks sixty. He has syphilis, and refuses to take medical advice. He walks the beaches around Arcachon with his pet cormorant on a leash—it walks with the same limp as its master. His friends say he is raving. At a loss for what to do, the family has him committed. At the end of one of the dim, narrow corridors in the Folie Saint-James Sanatorium stand two adjacent cells: Lautrec is put in one, his minder in the other. He writes to his father: "Anything that is not free, dies. You told me so, Father." Each day he is taken for thirty-minute walks in the grounds, but the only company to be had there is that of shawled consumptives, and they, like him, wheeze with every labored footstep, or just stand counting the fir trees along the perimeter. To prove he is better, he asks for materials so he can work: his liberty in exchange for pictures of circus horses. In March 1901 a brain hemorrhage leaves him paralyzed from the waist down. He is taken to the castle at Malromé, in La Gironde. His friends do not come to see him: La Gironde is a long way, in every respect, from the existence of the aesthetes and hedonists of fin de siècle Paris. Count Alphonse is the only one to spend the occasional hour at his bedside, coming by after returning from hunting; he sits absentmindedly shooting down flies with a sling made from his shoelaces.

One hot night, Lautrec dreams of his sorrel mare. The animal makes its way dolefully along the castle hallways, tossing its head and whinnying. The sound of its hoof-fall echoes off the stone floors as it comes through rooms of stifling Louis XIII tapestries, picks its way between furniture, past tables crammed with bibelots, and arrives at his bed. Its nostrils flare, an inch from the invalid's face, while its almond-colored tail ruffles the canopy. The painter dreams of waking, and that he finds the horse in the room with him. "Oh! Life, life!" he murmurs, trying, with legs that no longer respond, to kick off the sheets.

A LIFE IN PICTURES

I feel scared. I'm in the waiting room at my doctor's office, sitting on one of the plastic chairs. It's a cold spring morning. I made the appointment after several days with a constant vibration in my right eye. It vibrates, flickers—with ludicrous intensity, especially the lower lid. At moments I feel like it's going to explode. I've already discounted the most obvious causes: it can't be tiredness, because sometimes it kicks in barely five minutes after I wake; it can't be eyestrain, because I haven't read a single word in the last week. It isn't alcohol or cigarettes or coffee: I am an ascetic in all such matters. And as for stress—I don't believe in stress.

I considered possible illnesses. I went online and discovered that there are forums for people whose eyes vibrate. I was invited to attend a weekly meeting in the basement of the Bauen Hotel. These sessions involve sitting in a circle to share the array of associated psychological torments: chronic melancholia, morbid thoughts, migraines, sensations of unreality. They invite certain celebrity sufferers of "mad eye" to talk about their experiences: What did they do to prevent this inner tremor from being caught on camera? Thanks but no thanks, I said, and, sensing that things could really unravel if I carried on in this direction, called the doctor's.

The waiting room is immaculately white. A mother and her son are sitting across from me. The boy, who has thick glasses on, is chewing gum, and when he sees me looking he pulls out one end, elongating the white mass to form a looping, swaying bridge. The mother tells him to stop, but he carries on, and I eventually look away. My eye has started up again, for the hundredth time today. Then I see the Rothko: a reproduction poster on one of the walls. I see it and then quickly look down: if I look at any single thing for long the vibrations become more like a bombardment, like hooves galloping. It is one of Rothko's red pictures, one of the taller, thinner ones, and I recognize it from the National Museum of Fine Arts. A Rothko classic: a red devil on a burgundy background, veering into black.

People never tire of saying that you have to see original Rothkos, or nothing: that everything is lost in reproduction. But I find a surprising amount in these duplicates. They still give a sense of work that seeps into you bodily, not so much through your eyes as like a fire at stomach level. At points it even seems to me that Rothko creates not so much works of art as smoldering, endless blocks of fire, akin to the burning bush from Exodus. Something inexhaustible. And this is in spite of its creator, and in spite of the inflated rhetoric that has for so long posited him as someone who made mere images of the afterlife, someone who could be neatly slotted into an idea of abstract art as a sequence of spiritual "trips," after Kandinsky. I am thinking about this when Dr. Adelman's secretary says he is ready to see me now.

To the south of St. Petersburg, in what is now Latvia, lies Daugavpils, formerly Dvinsk. At the turn of the twentieth century, under the tsarist regime, employment was scarce and young women were frequently forced into prostitution. To avoid such a fate, a fifteen-year-old named Anna Goldin agreed to marry Jacob Rothkowitz, a local pharmacist. She bore him four children. The youngest, Marcus, the future Rothko, the most sensitive, indeed hypochondriac among them, was the only one to learn the Talmud.

Though there is no historical evidence of executions taking place in Dvinsk, in later years Rothko spoke of seeing a group of Cossacks taking Jews into the surrounding woods to dig a communal grave: "I saw that square grave in the woods so vividly that, though I can't be sure the massacre happened in my lifetime, I have always been haunted by the image." One morning Mrs. Rothkowitz and her children boarded a boat at the port of Liepāja. They were bound for the United States, where they were due to join the father, who had gone ahead a number of months before. The ship docked in Portland, Oregon, and they had barely set foot on shore when Mr. Rothkowitz died of cancer of the colon. Marcus was eleven years old: he was poor and Jewish, and left-leaning in his sense of politics. He made the best fist he could of high school, at the end of which he won a scholarship to study law at Yale in 1929. A few months later, as the Wall Street Crash began to eat away at the foundations of national life, he abandoned his studies. He had decided to give New York City a go, to "bum around and starve a bit."

Had he died at that point, history would not have remembered him, since before the age of forty-five, Rothko did nothing to distinguish himself as a painter. He had a Surrealist phase, a surprisingly mediocre one, and began in the 1930s to produce anguished cityscapes, complete with Giacometti-like elongated figures—hopeless.

One day he had the kind of moment that artists await their entire lives, and that sometimes comes, sometimes doesn't: the vision that finally brings them up from the depths. It came to Rothko in the summer of 1945, while he was in the process of setting down on canvas a series of abstract, blurry blocks of color floating in space. All notion of line and detail had disappeared, and color itself exploded: pinks, peaches, lavenders, whites, yellows, and saffron, as evanescent as steam on glass. It was as though his eyes had dilated.

People say you have to approach a Rothko in the same way you approach a sunrise. The work has a clear beauty, but that beauty can be either sublime or decorative. The canvases went well with the leather sofas and mohair rugs of Upper East Side living rooms. Critics hated them; Rothko endured their opprobrium while his bank balance swelled. He was accused of gimmickry, of making a buck from the reputation for rigor that Expressionism had forged. He came out in his own defense: "The experience of tragedy is for me the single source of art." Such grandiloquence, though, only stifled his paintings, making opaque menhirs of them.

But when Rothko felt anxious, he became talkative—overly so. And this in turn led him to overlook the fact that often the most powerful aspect of any work of art is its silence, and that—as they say—style is a medium in itself, its own means of emphasis. Perhaps there is something spiritual in the experience of looking at a Rothko, but it's the kind of spiritual that resists description: like seeing a glacier, or crossing a desert. Rarely do the inadequacies of language become so patently obvious. Standing before a Rothko, you might reach for something meaningful to say, only to end up talking nonsense. All you really want to say is "fuck me."

The years of his greatest success, from 1949 to 1964, coincided with Rothko's life unraveling: his marriage fell apart, his friends got as far away from him as they could, he drank just about anything he could get his hands on and became racked with hatred. He was on his way down, the spiral tightening. One stormy night, as he went to leave his apartment building, the porter told him to take care in the foul weather. To this Rothko said: "There's only one thing I need to take care of: stopping the black from swallowing the red."

"Had anything like this before?" says Dr. Adelman.

"In my eyes? Diplopia. I was going to have an operation when I was seven, but they couldn't do it: I was so nervous that the anesthetic didn't work. I was a wreck as a little girl, a bundle of nerves. Lucky that people change, right?"

Dr. Adelman, not answering this particular question, sends me back out to the waiting room.

I am supposed to keep my eyes shut until the drops take effect. I cheat, of course, I can't help it, peeking out at intervals between wet eyelashes. I look at the Rothko poster. I feel my pupils dilate. I shut my eyes. And when I open them again, again the red tries to engulf me; shut them and I see it floating on the back (black) of my eyelids. I get up and go over to it, see if I can stop exactly 18 inches away, which Rothko claimed was the optimal distance from which to view his work. How was it, I ask myself, that this man succeeded in creating such euphorically abstract images when his life was at its nadir? I think of T. S. Eliot: "The more perfect the artist, the more completely separate in him will be the man who suffers and the mind that creates." Dr. Adelman's secretary sees me wandering around and tells me to sit. I walk back to my seat with eyes shut.

On the morning of February 25, 1970, Rothko went into his bathroom, removed his shoes, hung his trousers and shirt over the back of a chair, and slit his wrists. He had advanced emphysema. When his assistant found him he was lying on his back in a puddle of blood, arms outstretched. An hour later, when the police arrived, the puddle had become a pool of red—about the same size as one of his paintings.

He took with him certain secrets: why for example, in 1959, at the apogee of his career, he reneged on an agreement to create some murals for the Four Seasons restaurant in Manhattan's Seagram Building. Dore Ashton, who frequently spent time with Rothko in his studio, said the painter thought he had signed up to make murals for the staff cafeteria. Others claim this to be a lie, that Rothko knew perfectly well that they were intended for the lavish main restaurant. This being the most expensive commission in the history of Abstract Expressionism, a couple of his best friends became his great enemies when Barnett Newman and Clyfford Still accused him of prostituting his art. (Though as a friend of mine would say, "There's prostitution and prostitution.") Rothko had another idea, and on a transatlantic crossing that same year, making his way to Naples, he confided in the journalist John Fischer over copious amounts of whiskey. His master plan, he said, as their drinks slopped onto the deck in tourist class, was "to ruin the appetite of every son of a bitch who ever eats in that room with paintings that will make those rich bastards feel that they are trapped." He was thinking of Michelangelo's oppressive Laurentian

Library, which he had seen in Florence a number of years before and was planning to visit again on this trip. A few days later, in Pompeii, Rothko, along with his wife, Mell, and his daughter, Kate, and Fischer, too, who proved impossible to shake off, went to see the Villa dei Misteri. Rothko was taken with the prurient reds and blacks in the dining room dedicated to Dionysus, the perverse melding of the two colors. All this was in his head when, back in New York City, he took his wife for lunch at the newly opened Four Seasons. His paintings were yet to be hung there; he claimed he still had to put the finishing touches to them. The restaurant was awash with navy-blue Brooks Brothers suits and Stefano Ricci ties, pearl necklaces and ermine stoles. Rothko spooned gazpacho into his mouth while inspecting his surroundings. He stopped suddenly, spoon in midair, and asked Mell if she smelled something. “Like what?” she said. “Like rotten money,” said Rothko. Downing his cocktail, he pushed back the table and announced his intention to break the contract.

The murals that never made it as far as the Four Seasons are horizontal smears of dry blood on brown backgrounds. When photos of them came out in the press, everyone agreed that it was little surprise they had not ended up adorning the walls of such an establishment: these works were as dead-end as anyone had seen, leading directly nowhere. I couldn’t agree less. Rothko had imagined paintings that would be as welcome as shards of glass in your risotto: his own direct and unabashed way of unsettling U.S. society. "Actually, on second thought," he said to poor Mell, the longtime recipient of her husband's speeches, "what's the point. These people will never get it." That day in the Four Seasons, it dawned on Rothko that no matter what he painted, his work would all end up as mere baubles. Just another thing for bankers to acquire, like the pretty wives sitting at the tables around him.

Dr. Adelman assures me it's nothing serious. A twitch, an involuntary tremor in the muscle fibers caused by an irritation elsewhere. My eye stops vibrating. I'm going to live, I say to myself, I'm going to live! Waiting for the elevator to arrive, I take a final look at the Rothko poster. I stare at it. It gives me a feeling of my singularity: a clear sense of the brutal solitude of this slab of sweating flesh that is me. I'm alive, I remember, and I can't help but immediately feel saddened, like anytime happiness is promised and you embrace it, but you know it isn't going to last.

My husband fell ill twice. Non-Hodgkin's lymphoma was the diagnosis. B cells the first time, the treatment long but relatively gentle; T cells the second, the treatment twice as long and utterly crushing. People say that if it happened to you, you'd find yourself fighting it; that everyone does. For my part, I doubt it. But he hung in there—in the Ramos Mejía Hospital to be precise, over a twelve-month period. Nights like tunnels, a pleurisy on his chest, chemo treatments that laid waste to his body; a litany of awful moments that I'll spare the reader. There was a prostitute at the hospital: very dark-skinned and always wearing a red dress and fishnet stockings, she spent the days asleep on the chairs in the reception area, nestled in among plastic bags that I suppose contained her worldly belongings. You'd see her shudder violently every now and then, as though a lightning bolt had passed through her. At night she could be heard walking the wards, her bare feet slapping against the icy floor tiles: she went from patient to patient, rubbing herself against the metal rails of the beds, doing whatever was required.

My husband had a small reproduction Rothko on the wall next to his oxygen tank. Other pictures too: a photo of his rock band, a postcard of the voluptuous '60s star Isabel Sarli, a napkin bearing the signature of the great football player Enzo "The Prince" Francescoli. It was me who brought the Rothko; the others had been brought by friends, in attempts to lift his spirits. They worked like pictures of saints, he said, particularly at night when the silence of the hospital started to weigh on him. "Sometimes

I press the morphine button and use my flashlight to look at them. That's quite good."

One night after I had stayed with him until late, it would have been around eleven in the evening, the prostitute came past, stopping at the foot of his bed. She said hello to my husband—she knew his name—and stood for a few moments looking at the pictures; there was a window beside the bed, and moonlight flooded the space. "Was I imagining it, or did she recognize the painting?" I asked my husband after she'd gone. "You weren't imagining it; she and I were chatting the other day, she says Rothko's her favorite painter now." Two nights after that I ran into her again. We were both standing waiting for the elevator, but it had stopped at the floor above and didn't seem like it was ever going to come. As we stood there, I gave her a smile, tried to act very cool. I was intrigued by her interest in Rothko, a most literal link between art and a life on the street. But she refused to return my gaze, and in so doing put me in my place: bourgeois art girl, hospital tourist, armchair anthropologist with a liking for the exotic. I took the hint, averted my eyes. When the elevator finally came, we rode it to the ground floor in silence, exiting into the large central hall that runs between the various wings and the reception area. She stepped out of the lift ahead of me, and for a brief moment I had the sensation that she was showing me the way to a chapel, to some place where a sacrifice or communion was going to take place. But then she immediately turned down an unlit hallway that led to Hematology. Her dress was the last thing I saw, in the precise moment when red dissolved into black.

BEAUTIFUL SHOCKS

Uncle Marion stepped out of the Monte Carlo casino at dawn, bleary-eyed, squinting in the early light, when a gunshot rang out on the terrace. Then he was awake. By the time he made it across the gardens to the Garnier fountain the body in its white linen suit was drifting like a water lily across the still surface of the basin. Marion thought it strange that the jets were off—he would have thought they stayed on permanently—but he later found out that this was normal procedure between five and nine in the morning to prevent the motors from overheating. A Tunisian doorman shrugged and called an ambulance, but it was slow arriving. The paramedics were tired of having to gather up these suicidal dawn gamblers.

I heard Uncle Marion tell this story at a dinner one evening in my family's apartment. I was hiding under the table, and it wasn't difficult to picture the sparkle in his eye. Incorrigible Marion. That was the last time I saw him; he died a few years later. He was my mother's uncle, and my godfather; my mother was no slouch when it came to such decisions, and knew it could pay to be high up in Marion's list of legatees. The inheritance turned out to be less spectacular than anticipated, though it was still greatly appreciated by me: three boxes of books, including some erotic picture cards by Aubrey Beardsley and an anthology of love letters by nineteenth-century writers over which I trembled whole nights at a time. The rest of the inheritance, the serious money and the land, was divided up among the siblings; the country house, meanwhile, was left to one of Marion's "nephews," as my parents, with an arch of the eyebrow, used to call his lovers. The siblings, all having hoped for a bigger slice, had no compunction about venting their anger at one another in claim and counterclaim over who had done the most for the old man. Nothing compares with the passions unleashed by a contested inheritance among a family still clinging on to millionaire pretensions, still struggling to accept its diminished lot. But I took sustenance from all the stories that came out about Marion then, stories about his eccentricities and heresies, nothing to do with acreages or legacies.

From my position beneath the table, I watched the forest of feet, high heels alternating with men's polished black shoes, and tried to decipher their language (if someone stamped on someone else's foot, that meant one thing; if one began taking off another's shoe, that meant something else). I listened in as the adults held forth. It was like the soothing sound of rain on windows, my favorite lullaby, reassuring confirmation that the world was still going on even as I turned away from it. Even now the sound of voices outside my window helps me to sleep. And the lower and more conspiratorial their voices grew, the better I was able to hear. As the after-dinner coffee grew cold, my parents and their friends swapped their Uncle Marion anecdotes, stories of him importing Moroccan gowns, of his attempts to establish a bird sanctuary at a lake outside Buenos Aires, and of time he spent in Venice: the gracefulness of the *gondolieri* had apparently affected his nerves. I had little idea what they were talking about, but when the guests left and Mama sent me up to bed I climbed the stairs with the indelible image of a middle-aged man dressed in a radiant blue gown picking his way through the reed bed of a lake. The gown was so brilliant, so refulgent, that the swans, herons, flamingos, and otters all stopped what they were doing to watch him go by. It wasn't until several years later that I came to a fuller understanding of this figure.

We visited the grave in Recoleta one morning, and Marion's sister Pepita, who was partially sighted, joined us. Afterward, partly in thanks to me for having been her guide dog and partly in an attempt to heal family wounds, she mentioned some things that began to bring him into focus:

"Do you know what happens if you draw a line in the ground around a hen? It'll become agitated, start flapping its wings, and so on, but it'll never cross that line—even just a faint line in the dirt with your toe. That's how it was with Marion. His whole life he desperately wanted to cut those ties—invisible class ties. Hence why he led one life in Buenos Aires, for Mama and Papa's benefit, and a completely different one abroad and away from the city, about which we were almost entirely in the dark. For example, when he was eighteen he fell in with a group of young men in the village. He met them at the tavern by the station, where all the laborers and fruit pickers went. It's astonishing that he got them to accept him at all, but I do know they loved the stories he told, and that he doled out bottles of Yardley cologne for them to wear instead of the cheap stuff. And my goodness, could he spin a yarn. His favorite story was about a crossing on board the *Cap*

Arcona and how, when they came to cross the equator, the captain stopped the ship and had oil dropped into the sea to give Anna Pavlova a steady platform to do the Dying Swan. He mesmerized them with tales from that time; to them it was like having a Martian land and getting to find out about life on other planets."

She tried to hide it, but I saw Pepita drying a tear that had welled inside her dark glasses. She moved on to a summer when the rest of the family went back to Buenos Aires from the countryside, but Marion stayed on alone:

"He'd brought back some fabrics from Paris, multicolored, like Pucci but in the days before Pucci, and he took them to Hilda, the village seamstress. Hilda must have thought he was mad, but he was so charming that she went along with it anyway. Marion could've charmed the hind ends off a herd of stampeding elephants if the mood took him. A week later he was presented with a mound of women's bathing costumes, frills everywhere, even the shoulder straps had frills on them. Marion laid them out on his bed and gave each one a name—Cacho, Centeno, Pirca, Rubén—keeping the prettiest one, made of a shimmering blue fabric, for himself. He then sent a horse and cart to the village and asked for young men to be brought. They were promised as much champagne as they could drink and a barbecue fit for kings, and when fifteen of them arrived, that's exactly what they got. They were having a fine time, drunk as lords, and when nightfall came, out came the swimming costumes. They emerged one by one from the little changing hut by the pool, and it was like someone had opened the cages at the zoo. Can you imagine: fifteen of these strapping young guys, dressed in girls' swimsuits, prancing around the side of the pool, flapping their arms like they were about to take off. It must have been some sight. People always said my brother was unusual. I wish. Unusual isn't that far away from completely normal; unusual you can house-train. But Marion needed, how can I say it . . . he needed to have these *beautiful shocks* in his life. He had to have them. Otherwise he'd wither and die. By the time he went off to the country house, he was like a lion that'd had its teeth removed, but before that . . . I sometimes found his escapades hard to stomach, but he'd always just laugh and recite a line from Jacques Esprit, a guiding spirit for him: 'When it comes to men, my dear Pepita, their virtues are far more perverse than their vices.'"

The boudoir in the Errázuriz Palace was for the oldest son in the family. It was intended as an exact replica of his father's study: a Louis XVI–style private reception room, the walls suffocated in burgundy. But the young Matías Errázuriz, later to become my uncle Marion, asked to take charge of the decorations himself. He commissioned the Catalan artist Josep Maria Sert, who spent two years on the job. It is the property's most innovative space, or experience, I would say; a set of mental and physical sensations, more than anything, that for me reproduce what it must be like to be shut inside a cage. I do not know if Sert realized what he was doing. I tend to think that it was his wife, the legendary Misia Godebska, who oversaw the job; she knew better than anyone what it was to be a prisoner to luxury.

The walls are dark—you don't notice them. What jumps out at you is all the gold: the gold-leaf double doors, the golden picture frames, the heavy golden lampshades hanging down from the lattice of roof beams, also golden. Each wall has an oil painting of a different carnival scene, bursting nightmarishly with harlequins, Buddha figures, and transvestites, easily as bizarre as anything by Léon Bakst. The whole of human comedy is here: the great farcical masque of society seen from the inside of a cage. The museum catalogue claims that the pictures offer a critique of decadence, but Matías Errázuriz was eighteen when he commissioned them, an age at which anyone born with even the slightest leaning toward the outlandish is less likely to moralize than to want to set fire to the moralizers.

Come in, come in: over here we see Matías Errázuriz sitting in his boudoir. A couple of female acquaintances are with him, and they are drinking together, and the cigarette smoke drifts up, covering Sert's paintings in a gauzy fog. The laughter grows louder as the night wears on. One of the women, in a black dress, sprawls languidly on a chaise longue.

"Do not move!" says Matías. "That is exactly how Misia was, in that exact same position, when I met her."

"Is she as beautiful as everyone says?"

"Depending on how the light falls, she can be quite lovely or fairly plain, but what she has is the most disarming elegance . . . The truth is I only got Sert in so I could have a little bit of Misia. I sometimes think I catch her perfume floating on the air in here."

"And what about him?"

"Sert? Don't get me started. A Catalan drama queen. All the ambition of a Renaissance painter—all the body odor, too. In Paris they call him the Tiepolo of the Ritz, for his murals . . . I know his work verges on the baroque, but he's better with small commissions. When I saw what he did with the Countess of Bearn's mansion, I thought I was going to die."

"Darling! You should have brought him to Buenos Aires."

"Darling, I tried. But Misia has a fear of boats, she's terrified of the things. The only place she'll go is Italy. She says the art's worth the agony of getting there."

"And didn't she meet Sert in Italy?"

"A little before, I think, in Paris. But they had an early dalliance at the Grand in Rome. She was getting away from her second husband, a man about as jealous as a Barbary pigeon. He'd go out to buy her jewelry, and leave her locked in her room. Misia was his greatest acquisition. He bought her from her first husband, Natanson, the founder of *La Revue Blanche*. Literally, he bought her."

"You do lay it on, Matías."

"I do not. Natanson was in so much debt, Misia was the only thing he had left to pawn. He was a pushover, real jellyfish, but he was also the first to appreciate what a good eye Misia had. After that, everyone wanted her approval. She was the godmother of Diaghilev's Ballets Russes, Proust wrote to her—one long parenthesis! Bonnard gave her some screens which she adapted to fit the shape of her dining room—he loved her even more after that! You know how many of Toulouse-Lautrec's pictures she swept out of her kitchen along with the dinner crumbs? Pictures 'dedicated to the Swallow'—her very own pet name. When people told her she was a fool for not keeping them, she said, 'Keep them? Would you try to bottle the rays of the sun?'"

"They can't have been much good."

"Good, bad, what kind of gauge is that?" says Matías. "Either one likes a thing, or one does not. That is all. Now, get your lips around this mint julep and try telling me it isn't art."

A cage is a strange thing, perverse even: it isn't that you suffocate inside it, rather you get used to living off the minimum amount of air possible. That was how Misia lived, picking her words as though she had to be careful about the amount of air that went in and out of her lungs. "She always breathed out extremely gently," recalled Uncle Marion, "like she'd taken lessons from Beethoven in the art of breathing." Misia would oversee salon discussions, private affairs that were at the same time highly impersonal; not so much circling as orbiting any true intimacy at great distance. Not even Uncle Marion could have imagined how Misia would end her days—no one could. No one actually knew where she came from—not even Uncle Marion.

When her mother, Zofia, was eight months pregnant with her, an unsigned letter arrived from St. Petersburg informing her that her husband, Cyprian, was the father of the child expected by Princess Yusupova, a belle who would cause a commotion in the salons of the capital by showing up with a pair of wolves on leashes. Zofia needed to hear this from her husband. It was winter, and the journey all but impossible for someone that far along, but she undertook it nonetheless, and when she arrived she went to his room at the Hotel Nevsky, only to find him out on some assignation. She waited and waited, and when finally he deigned to appear, Zofia lay dead on the bed; the midwife beside her held out his crying baby. The child was christened Misia and sent to Brussels to live with her paternal grandmother, a hardened alcoholic who used to dip her breakfast bun in a glass of chartreuse.

Her aunt Ursula lived in the Brussels mansion too. One afternoon when the family car broke down Ursula took the tram to go shopping. It was her first experience of public transport and—perhaps it was the shock of the new—the very moment she set eyes on the tram driver she felt a lightning bolt split her in two. From that second on, her single desire was to see him again. When she realized the relationship was an impossibility, she shut herself in her room and stopped eating. The blinds lowered, she rolled herself up in a fetal ball next to one of the walls and was dead within three weeks. Her knees were pressed so rigidly against her chest that they had to snap the leg bones to put her death shroud on and fit her in the coffin.

Her mother and her aunt had shown Misia that love was a dark thing, best avoided. Sert was the only one who made her feel like ignoring the family lessons. Within ten minutes of their meeting in a Rome hotel, the Catalan whisked her out for a walk in the grounds. They came to a lake with a pair of swans in it; the birds' wings had been clipped so that the hotel guests could admire them at close quarters all year round. Misia was taken aback, but Sert, in the unmistakably husky tones of the charlatan and imposter, whispered in her ear: "They are happy in their jail, my girl." And Misia, too, was happy for a time, moving through apartments she herself designed—Sert doing her bidding—and then abandoning them like empty perches. When war broke out, that was an end to all the parties. Misia turned to antidepressants; morphine, in those days. Meanwhile, Sert had fallen for Roussy Mdivani, a Georgian princess of orchidlike beauty who had originally come to him looking for an art tutor. For Misia the choice was either be tossed aside or join a ménage à trois, and she went for the latter. Together the trio visited Baroness Erlanger's Villa Foscari in the countryside near Venice, the work of the architect Andrea Palladio and one of the most melancholic buildings in the world. It was virtually unfurnished, and the baroness, who lived there with her lover and her children, spent day and night scraping back the limewash on the walls, hoping to uncover the Veronese frescoes supposedly hidden underneath. Sert sank down into a sofa and peered admiringly up at the ceilings through his monocle, while his two women fussed around him.

And then the worst happened: rather than dying from heartache, Misia went on to outlive both Sert and Roussy Mdivani. She stopped going out. When going out was unavoidable, she would do so only at night, in order to be able to inject the morphine under her moiré dress without anyone seeing. It must have been around this time that a famous photograph was taken of her in Venice—"refuge of endless strange secrets, broken fortunes and wounded hearts," as Henry James put it—the city in which, wherever you lay your hand, it comes up smeared with gold. It was the winter of 1947, and St. Mark's Square stood frozen and deserted, except for the figure of Misia wrapped in a greatcoat but shivering nonetheless, her high heels accentuating her lapwing legs. The cage door was open but Misia had forgotten how to fly away: she had lost her sense of direction.

Marion went to visit his nieces and nephews in the countryside every summer. "This was where he used to get off the train," my mother told me sixty years later, pointing to a field in which a number of Hereford cows were grazing, considering us with a vacancy of expression found only in cattle and in poets in their reveries.

"But where's the station?" we said.

"He didn't need one," she said. "If you tipped well

enough, you could get down where you liked. When are you going to get your heads around it? The world was *theirs.*"

Picture a sunrise, a field, and a man of about thirty stepping off a train in the middle of that field. The guard has brought some wooden steps especially for him. His suit has an English cut, and he wafts away the morning flies with a white muslin handkerchief. He carries himself like a king in exile; you half expect to see a couple of greyhounds trailing after him. Instead he has a leather suitcase, covered in stickers, and a hummingbird in a cage. Each year he brings his nieces the same gift, and each year what follows is the same; these girls, however, still believe in miracles.

The three nieces jump down from the small carriage and, their mother looking on with the reins in her hands, go rushing over to him. Marion kneels down in the tufty, dew-covered grass and lets himself be engulfed.

"You came to get me, all of you! Sweet things. I might be mistaken, but could it be *this* you're after?" he says, the girls already beginning to squabble over the birdcage.

From the carriage, their mother calls out to her brother.

"I love those trousers, dear! Are they new? Wonderful you could make it, though I do worry we'll bore you. How was the city? Any of your lot still around?"

Marion comes over and, smiling wickedly, kisses his sister on both cheeks.

"It's you who looks fabulous! Quite the country lady."

They each know this game: tongues both sharp and silken. He gets in the front next to his sister, the girls squeeze into the back, a blanket over their knees in the fresh early morning air; the cage rests atop the blanket. The house is a little under a mile away, and they have to take it in turns to hold the cage; inside, the hummingbird flits about, unsettled by the motion of the carriage. The battered wheels lift golden clouds of dust into the air.

The mother stops in front of the house and the girls run inside with the cage, taking it into the living room and placing it by a corner window on a game table whose top doubles as a backgammon board and a cover for a roulette wheel that they are forbidden to use. Up in his room, Marion places his suitcase on the bed, opens it, and takes out his aquamarine silk pajamas, Moroccan slippers, and lavender cologne. He hears his nieces racing along the hall. Back and forth they go, bringing water and birdseed, and whooping and shouting, a whole gamut of joyful noises, like a pianist doing scales.

After lunch the younger children are dragged off to have a siesta. This is the first year that the oldest has been exempt from this enforced daily death, and she uses the time alone to spy on the hummingbird. The iridescent sheen of its feathers makes her stomach flutter. Long, thin fingers slip in through the bars, but she can't quite reach it. She nudges pieces of milky bread closer with a cocktail stick as the bird throws its beak nervously from side to side. Unmoving, elbows up on the baize, the girl spends a long time gazing in; she is evaluating the likelihood of success, the probability of a miracle. These are her thoughts until she hears footsteps behind her, at which her guard goes up. Not that she is startled, she does not even turn around—she has been expecting it. When the scent of lavender comes close, this girl who will later become my mother says in a very low voice, almost to herself:

"This one's going to live, isn't it, Uncle Marion?"

THE HILLS FROM YOUR WINDOW

One day, you develop a fear of flying. Apropos of nothing. It's your age, must be. Before you turned twenty-five, flying seemed the most natural way to go from one place to another. But now the mere thought sends you into a panic, and it's beyond you how you're going to board the plane you're supposed to be taking to Geneva. An art convention awaits you in the cathedral of money: a foundation has invited the curator of the Venice Biennale, the director of New York's PS1, a critic from *Artforum*, along with a few others. Your inclusion in the jury is an error, you're sure. But when they told you about the honorarium, it didn't seem very clever to point this out, considering the state of your bank account at the time. (The state of your bank account always.) Plus the job could hardly have been easier: just suggest an artist, someone young and Latin American whose work would benefit from a push. Because you don't travel, you decided to pick someone from Argentina. You did feel guilty and took a ferry over the border to Montevideo to have a scout around there. Still, no more plain sailing for you now, no getting out of this one: fly to Switzerland, join the rest of the jury, help pick a winner from the nominees. Someone is going to be awarded a grant that will likely change the course of their entire career.

An artistic education? The idea hasn't even occurred to Henri Rousseau, a young man from the town of Laval in western France. No matter: according to Courbet, painting cannot be taught anyway. Except Henri doesn't know who Courbet is yet. He doesn't know much of anything, except for how to hammer sheets of steel until they are thin as communion wafers. His father is the town tinsmith, and Henri plans to follow in his footsteps. It is a job he takes seriously. He has his father's somber air, if not the same capacity for daydreaming. But when his father dies suddenly, before passing on anything but the rudiments of the job, Henri takes work as an errand boy at a local law firm. Some rubber stamps go missing from the office one night, and the new boy is the prime suspect. He decides to enlist as a way of avoiding the repercussions. War has broken out, and the army is recruiting.

Bismarck's forces lay siege to Paris. Rousseau writes to his mother, who has moved to the capital, but he has no way of getting the letters to her. A fellow soldier tells him that food has become so scarce that they've begun raiding the city zoo; one restaurant is said to have been serving elephant soup and antelope terrine. Rumors and hearsay are the extent of the information they receive, because the Germans are intercepting all mail, magazines and newspapers as well as letters and cables. But the sun comes out one afternoon, and a solitary cloud is seen to hang over the Prussian lines; Corporal Rousseau, shielding his eyes, discerns that the cloud is moving faster than seems normal, and its shape isn't quite right, more like an Easter egg than a cloud. No, now he sees: it's a hot-air balloon. He's never seen one before. He looks on in raptures until, minutes later, the trailing guide-rope catches on the bell tower of a church, and the balloon collapses like a calf lassoed in a rodeo. As it deflates, he manages to make out the name on the canvas: *Victor Hugo*. In the following months more than seventy hot-air balloons are sent over from Montmartre bearing mail, and cages; the soldiers send letters back via pigeon post, writing their missives on rolled-up microfilm that is then tied to the birds' legs. The Prussians bring hawks, and begin trying to intercept the messages that way.

Your husband goes with you to Ezeiza International. In the airport bar, while you fiddle with a paper napkin, he says you need to fight it together. You nod. The relationship has entered a cooler, duller phase. After ten years together, he is still the best person you know, but you are still so immature. *If the thrill is gone*, you keep thinking. You think about yourself, in other words, even in matters of the heart. You fold up the napkin, making an origami bird, then notice the words *Dolce vita, tu vita* written in black. Not a good omen, you think. You present him with the bird. He hands back the Klonopin: white, surprisingly small. "Is this really going to do it?" you ask, but he doesn't reply. You break it in half and swallow it with some water. Ten minutes later, the other half. You have never taken downers, and assumed it would completely capsize you, but an hour passes and you feel nothing—except the downward pressure in your chest, sweat on your palms, and your heart going a million beats a minute. So exactly how you felt before. Once you've made it through customs, you find a pay phone and call your brother. He's a pilot, and should surely have some reassuring words, but what does he come up with? "If you actually stop to think about the physics of it, flying in an airplane is the most insane thing ever." You understand why young people find it exciting, but fully grown adults? What happens if you change your mind and want to get off? Sure, right now—that's Cape Verde down there. What's going on? Why are they looking at me like that? You guys are the weirdos, choosing between in-flight meals, not even blinking when they bring out those mini wine bottles. Clinking glasses and *sharing the moment* like you're in some expensive restaurant. Guys, you are in the sky. In. The. Sky. If we were meant for this, we'd have been made with wings. Wings sprouting out of our shoulder blades, yes? Plenty of space to pin a pair of wings there, see? Oh, plenty of space.

At the age of forty-five, and mired in an unnameable sadness, Rousseau turns to painting. Five of his seven children have died of tuberculosis, and painting becomes his way of regaining the paradise he has lost. At first he is content to be a Sunday painter, but he soon gains permission to work in the Louvre. On either side of him, ranked students from the Académie produce faithful copies of what they see; Rousseau copies too, but never faithfully. During the rest of the week he works as a tax collector in Paris's toll stations. People begin calling him the Taxman.

The images he conjures have the freshness, the verve, of a six-year-old's imagination. The Sundays come and the Sundays go, and those qualities show no sign of abating. "Wondrous Rousseau," pronounces Alfred Jarry when he comes to see his work. This is the Rousseau everyone knows, the unadulterated talent, painter of fluorescent jungle scenes, wild beasts, and enigmatic, sphinxlike women. But another Rousseau exists, one more attached to his city and its forms. The man in thrall to flying machines. Many of his smaller works feature not only hot-air balloons, but Zeppelins and airplanes too. Only one of these has an aircraft seen not from the ground: *Portrait of My Father*, which is held in Argentina's National Museum of Fine Arts. The elongated framing, the clouds we find ourselves level with, and the romantic aura that impregnates the scene all combine to suggest an elevated point of view. Not bird's-eye, but looking out as if from the basket of a hot-air balloon as it rises vertically into the sky.

"The cloud inside a paper bag" was a thing of such beauty that it made people gasp, but it was also entirely useless, the definition of "art for art's sake," as Benjamin Constant noted in his diary on February 11, 1804. The hot-air balloon had begun life as a visual poem, though not at the hands of a poet; rather, a hen and a sheep were the first passengers ever to board one belonging to the Montgolfier brothers. Men came later. Up they went, drunk on adrenaline and champagne, bottles of which were indispensable fuel for every flight as well as the last bits of ballast to be dropped if greater altitude was desired. At the end of the nineteenth century, the aviator was the flâneur of the firmament, and a trip in a hot-air balloon was seen to be just as health-giving as a hotel in the mountains. Well, nearly. You just had to watch out for telegraph wires (decapitation hazards), the manic variability of the wind (that indomitable colt), not going too high (wouldn't want to run out of oxygen), or coming home too late (one account from the time talks about the claustrophobic sensation of flying over fields at night, which would of course have lain in total darkness, as being "like traversing a slab of black marble"). It was relatively simple to land, although the basket would sometimes bounce a few times, toadlike, before stopping. People often came away with bumps and bruises, but that didn't stop them wanting to fly again. Nobody denied the dangers, because of the obvious and significant spiritual benefits of gaining that kind of elevation: seen from above, the earth, and all earthly concerns, took on their true dimensions.

When you were in the air you forgot your troubles. Rousseau, though, not having the chance to go up himself, had to make do with imagining what that would be like. The French Cloudgazing Society, a clandestine group that met on the terrace of the Paris Physics Institute, and with which Rousseau had some association, contended: "Clouds have been unjustly stigmatized. We are against the praise of blue skies." Rousseau dreamed of going up, up, up—and then coming face-to-face with his father. Might his children be somewhere up there too? Would cirrus clouds bring the most apparitions, or cumulonimbus? At times he framed the question more existentially: Could there exist a God lost in time, some entity that might provide the answers he sought?

His indifference to worldly matters made him equally unconcerned about success and failure. Rousseau wasn't naïve, but aloof, and with good reason: he had come to realize that his inner skies were far more refined than the rarefied climes of vanguardist salons. His evasiveness irked some people. At the end of Picasso's famous dinner in his honor, all the guests stood to applaud the brilliance of the Taxman, and tears were flowing freely as they led him out to his car—only for Picasso, with the cruelty of all true cowards, to confess that the whole thing had been a joke, *une blague*. The same Picasso, this was, who would go on to hoard Rousseau's work like bottles of Coca-Cola in the desert, and who twenty years later, when doing his preparations for *Guernica*, shut himself in his studio to study *The War*, but never admitted it in public. The avant-garde took more from Rousseau than he ever took from it. You would have expected Rousseau to pick up the occasional tic or tendency from the leading lights of his time, but far from it.

Rousseau's jungles appear otherworldly, though only until we see that this far-off planet is also our own. Suddenly magazines in Europe were bringing exotic images into the public consciousness, publications such as *Le Magasin pittoresque* or *Le Journal des voyages* presenting images nobody could otherwise have dreamed. The fascination with the exotic, soon to manifest in safaris, in Gauguin's move to Tahiti, and in the market for tribal masks in Paris, was intrinsic in the spread of empire. Modern art was born with colonialism at its height, and images of Africa titillated the middle classes like little else. At the 1899 World's Fair, a group of Senegalese tribesmen were installed, huts and all, on the Esplanade des Invalides. The visiting crowds truly were flustered. Darwin's revelations to do with possible shared origins led some young French ladies to report tingling sensations between their legs. It was out of this turmoil that Rousseau's images arose; the closest he ever came to a jungle was among the palm trees, ficus, and winter ferns in the botanical gardens, and the closest to the sky when he read Jules Verne's *Five Weeks in a Balloon*.

•

You never got on the plane, never made it to Geneva. Your husband left you at the airport with your head swimming; it was you who asked him to leave, saying it felt like you were being watched. You grabbed your suitcase, went through the pantomime of checking in, took the escalator, conferring smiles on your fellow passengers all the while (as they say in show business, "Careful how you treat people on your way up, you might meet them on your way back down"), but when it came to placing your bag inside the metal detector, it struck you that there was another option. How about not laying your head on the block? You turned and walked back the way you had come, down the escalator, past families saying their goodbyes, smiling at everyone—though this time the smiles were genuine. You went outside and got in a taxi. You were home before your husband.

It was the most wayward thing you've done, in a life of following rules: standing up a dozen illustrious curators in Geneva. Them sitting at their mahogany table in an Alpine art institution; you feeling like Sid Vicious singing his version of "My Way." And best of all, your pick still won. Which only goes to show, when a piece of work is good, it doesn't need anyone or anything to help sell it.

Not traveling naturally means missing out on certain things. Forget about standing before *The Dream*, one of Rousseau's great works, held at MoMA and capable, they say, of making the earth move. Piero della Francesca's *Madonna del parto* is housed in Monterchi, Italy, and would apparently cause a German governess to emote. Or Fragonard's *Stolen Kiss*, in the Petersburg Hermitage; that will have to wait for some future Slavic reincarnation. And, for that matter, it's also time you gave up on ever partaking in Japanese *hanami* or "flower viewing," the spring celebration of the cherry trees coming into blossom.

You tell yourself that you'll still have imagination on your side, and you've got plenty at hand to keep you entertained. Take a bus, get off the bus, go into the museum, and walk, simply walk, straight to whichever picture is calling you. Easy, and easy on the purse, too. You know some of these works as well as you know the books on your shelves and the plants in your garden. When you step in front of Rousseau's portrait of his father, you greet him like a close relative: You're fine, but how is *he* today? You don't care what your own family says (though you do listen—to give yourself a stick to beat them with). Buenos Aires, they say, only has second-rate work: great artists, yes, but none of their great works. If you're serious about art, you have to travel. There's a Buzz Aldrin line that your mother is forever quoting to you, seemingly as often as she can: "Flying: it's the only way to see the world."

If only you could go off in a hot-air balloon! Hot-air balloons are the obverse of modern aeronautical advances, the beautiful black sheep to the success story of the airplane. One promises a romantic voyage, the other a global transfer. But, like the glowworms you used to see in childhood and now not at all, hot-air balloons just don't seem to be around anymore.

Who knows, though, maybe you've just convinced yourself, in line with your progressive and alarming tendency to limit your own means, that big planes and great works are unnecessary. Cézanne said, "The grandiose . . . grows tiresome after a while. There are mountains like that; when you stand before them you shout *Nom de Dieu*, but for every day a simple little hill does well enough." The city you live in is flat and gray, but the clouds occasionally part and, out of nowhere, something emerges. Days like today, when the skies are clear—you see it from your window. A low hilltop with thunderclouds brewing beyond it.

TO BE A RAPPER

I speak to my friend Fabiolo on the phone every week, but we see each other only once a year, if that, and then only to reassure ourselves that the other is still alive. Also, we seem to converse in soliloquies. I don't know if I'm guilty of this too, but increasingly it's as though Fabiolo, as soon as he's finished saying something, answers himself—mimicking my voice and my usual bad temper.

"Why do you call, if you don't want to listen at all?" I say (actually it's always me who calls him). Since Fabiolo always makes people leave a message (or maybe just makes me), I feel a pressure to come up with something good, some intrigue. There's nothing stopping me making up anything I like, and I have no qualms about lying—I abide by the reality-TV rule: as long as no children are harmed, anything goes. When Fabiolo gets around to calling back, I always start soft, asking, for example, what he's had for lunch, though I already know the answer: that unholy combination of sticky rice and boiled potatoes he feeds on day and night, making his body one of the true nutritional enigmas. I ask him if he's seen the doctor yet to ask about his stomach problems, the answer to which is always no. He hates doctors, he's interested only if one of them is going to promise him immortality. Niceties covered, we get into our flow, one or sometimes both of us boasting about recent exploits, or the latest instalment in our long-running argument over the pronunciation of "Somerset Maugham," and from there onto whatever we've been reading. "Tell me what you're reading and I'll tell you where your head's at," says Fabiolo. "Gogol," I admit. As will perhaps be apparent, we don't make for the happiest of couples. No matter what we start off with, it never takes long for us to move onto our two recurrent interests: childhood and old age. The pleasure we take in these is both morbid and very much evident. They are subjects we could mine endlessly.

"Beginnings and ends are everything," says Fabiolo. "The rest is noise. The middle is just the residue of what happens at either extremity; it lacks mystery."

“Speaking of which,” which is what I say when I sense he’s about to launch into one of his discourses, “did I tell you about the Schiavoni mystery?”

“Yes, a hundred times, but go ahead. I do nothing but repeat myself anyway.”

It was a rebound attraction—aren’t they always? I was going around the museum giving the well-known works a wide berth, fed up with all the twentieth-century pieces trying so hard, shouting so loudly about their own messianic significance, when a painting caught my eye. *Augusto Schiavoni*, said the panel. It didn’t ring any bells—I knew of a Schiavoni car mechanic, a Schiavoni moving company . . . And then there was the resemblance. The similarity sent a shiver down my spine and, now that I think of it, it must have been this that made the piece so arresting.

I heard a throat being cleared and looked around. A man was standing next to me, about forty years old, brown deck shoes, beige trousers, bluey-green Ralph Lauren jumper. A hundred to one he’s an architect, I thought, and promptly felt an urge to discuss the picture. I gave him a conspiratorial look, trying to guide his eyes straight back to the painting—not wanting him to get any ideas about assignations in this semideserted museum, at two o’clock on a weekday afternoon.

"Do you see what I see?"

"Oh, yes," he said, his accent such that I could immediately tell he drank only tea that came direct from London. "Poor show from the curators, shocking, really. Putting such a trifle next to something as majestic, as *suggestive*, as that." He nodded over at the adjacent Pettoruti.

Why can't I just keep my mouth shut? Dear God, not that you're listening, but where *do* you get them? The only company I like in a museum is that of primary school children. Though even that can be bittersweet: no sooner will they have formed their little semicircle on the floor, the teacher about to launch into some explanation, than their faces turn a drawn, sickly green; she has sat them down in front of a Velázquez. "Stop!" I feel like shouting. Carelessly administered, the history of art can be lethal as strychnine.

I had wanted to check whether I was seeing things. That was why I needed the architect, for a second opinion: the girl in the picture looked exactly like me, I thought, or me as an eleven-year-old. The same eyes as mine, wide-set, staring coldly back; the surly, boastful look. But I wasn't in the habit of carrying around photos of myself as a child, so there was nothing for the man to compare against. Plus I had doubts about my ability to explain anything to him, so absorbed had I become in the painting; it felt like it was just me and the girl in the room, as though all the figures around us, on her side of the canvas and mine, had been redacted with thick black daubs of paint. Her and me, me and her. Why deny it?—it was the sensation of seeing myself, a version of myself in need of affection, that had acted on me so strongly: I felt like running to the little girl in the picture and throwing my arms around her. I know, I know, this is about as far from hard-nosed criticism as you can get, but isn't all artwork—or all decent art—a mirror? Might a great painting not even reformulate the question *what is it about* to *what am I about*? Isn't theory also in some sense always autobiography?

I get goose bumps just thinking about this Schiavoni piece. I believe in the supernatural as an aspect of the intellect, by which I mean I don't see ghosts but I very much believe in the reality of them. I dragged Fabiolo along one day to see the Schiavoni. You need cunning if you're ever to make Fabiolo leave his house, and I picked a tender spot, somewhere I knew it would hurt. When I did finally tease him out of his bunker I showed him a photo of me in childhood. He looked back and forth between it and the picture, nodding. "Yes," he said, "I see it. Spooky!" Then again, it's hard to tell with Fabiolo. I have the sense that he's so open to the idea of the universe as inherently mysterious that there aren't really any eventualities he hasn't entertained. Maybe he saw a likeness, maybe he was just telling me what I wanted to hear so he could scurry back beneath his rock.

We've discussed the possibility of the girl in the picture being a distant relative, which would make the quest for answers a genetic one. We even wondered if it might be a case of souls transmigrating, to nervous laughter from both of us, until Fabiolo asked to change the subject; he is genuinely frightened of ghosts.

I would have loved to be the one to discover Schiavoni, but others got there first. Born in Rosario at the end of the nineteenth century, when he traveled to Italy in 1914 he was following a path that was by then obligatory for any Argentinian painter with a modicum of talent. He made the trip with Manuel Musto, his only friend in Rosario, a tortured painter who had lost his twin brother to pneumonia at the age of twelve. Both came from well-off families, and once in Florence they rented an opulent room with plenty of light. You could be mistaken for thinking the large window overlooked the sea, given the intensity of Schiavoni's gaze when he stood looking out of it.

They joined the workshop of Giovanni Costetti, a celebrated but mediocre painter. It was obvious that Schiavoni was searching for something that Costetti couldn't offer, but not even he knew what it was, nor was he willing to discuss it with anyone; he had realized that the only way to keep other people from spoiling one's innermost thoughts and yearnings was never to talk about them. The waiters and waitresses at the bars on either side of the Ponte Vecchio were to become his only confidants; as he sat watching them he became increasingly convinced that each resembled a different figure from classical painting, and soon there was nobody else he felt capable of opening up to. A waitress with a melancholic countenance—reminiscent of Andrea del Sarto's *Madonna delle Arpie*—was the one with whom Schiavoni finally spoke of the visions he'd been having. They had been to bed together and, as they sheltered from the rain in a dank alleyway, he felt open and tender. It was she who told him to go to Naná's salon.

The two friends arrived at the salon to find a room full of the bereaved; all had lost family members. Naná came out in a negligee with ostrich feathers splayed downward from the neck. Her skin was brilliantly, exuberantly white (though only at a distance; the thick layer of makeup became apparent close up). She did not speak—this only when the spirits came—but went around giving each of her guests a welcoming hug, clasping them to her like stray little calves. Schiavoni and Musto tried to steal looks at her sternum, where a scar was said to be. Naná's acolytes claimed that it was through this poorly executed piece of surgery that the souls of the dead crossed over.

On New Year's Eve five years earlier, a woman had appeared at the Ospedale degli Innocenti with an axe lodged in her chest. The doctors recognized her as a waitress from the tourist dives near the Porta del Paradiso. The woman was Naná, and she had miraculously avoided damage to her vital organs in the attack. They sewed the thorax back together with surgical wire, and had to work quickly because too little anesthetic had been administered and she began to talk in tongues: first in the gruff tones of a Sardo-Piedmontese cavalry soldier who had died at the Battle of Montebello and cursed the name of General Morelli di Popolo for sending them out on one-eyed horses; then, to the room's equal astonishment, Artemisia Gentileschi started speaking, begging to be recognized as the painter of *Judith Slaying Holofernes*, at which point the surgeons decided they'd had enough of this phantasmal chatterbox and sedated her once more, this time with a more generous dose. Naná never brought charges, either against her attacker or the hospital. Generally sanguine in outlook, she only complained at having missed the chance to try morphine, given her obvious intolerance to opiates.

And so a lowly waitress became the most famous medium in Florence. There was a clamor to get a look at the scar, the mystical opening. But Naná quickly realized that mystery was her greatest ally in this profession, and always covered it up with the feather-collar negligee. Only in the most intense sessions, when her body began to buck and tremble, would the garment fall open, revealing the dark vertical scar between her breasts: six inches long and a couple of inches wide.

To the Florentine waiters and waitresses she was St. Naná. Her story of hope, of the vanishing rarity that was social mobility, spread across the cafés and bars of the city. Her dealings with the dead had given her a way out. Some cast doubt on her ability to dematerialize as she was said to do, to admit these dead souls, but a contrary view tended to prevail: in the end, nobody was harmed by her visions. In some ways she was a model citizen, in that she at least served others.

On the evening of their visit Schiavoni and Musto sat down with the others at a circular table. A red silk cloth had been draped over the lamp, suffusing the space with a crimson gloom, while a stuffed owl scowled out at the new arrivals from the mantelpiece. The heavy velvet curtains were shut, and it was stuffy. Electricity passed from fingertip to fingertip as the guests joined hands, awaiting the arrival of the spirits.

"Who's there?" hissed Naná's assistant. "Is anyone present with us today?"

A knocking began on the table, at first with no apparent rhythm, but then, as the guests were invited to ask the spirit if it belonged to the person they wanted to contact, establishing a pattern: one knock for yes, two for no. Naná suddenly spoke, in a childish falsetto:

"Tomorrow's my twelfth birthday," it said, "but Mama is worried about my cough."

To Musto's horror—he'd had his arm twisted to come—he recognized his twin brother's voice. The pneumonia had taken him on the day he turned twelve. Naná ordered Musto to pick up a pencil and write down what she was about to say:

"Be Oedipus in your life, and the Sphinx will be your grave."

Musto was unconvinced. His brother might have sounded like that, but he didn't talk in riddles. A card-carrying positivist, he marched out of the session. But Schiavoni stayed, and kept on coming back. Why did his friend have to take it so seriously, he said? What was one more hollow phrase in a world full of them? All he knew was that the sessions did him good; anytime he felt himself beginning to plummet, he liked to go and sit in this red room and let life slip by. "You have the gift," Naná said to him one evening, after he admitted he had glimpsed a pair of ectoplasmic figures flanking each of her assistants. One was the adorable little child that each had been, and the other the dark monster they were bound to become.

Schiavoni had been receptive ever since he was a boy. Lying in his bed at night, he had learned to send himself into a trance by holding his breath long enough that he partially passed out. He began to enjoy leaving the world behind, and the risks paled in comparison with the consciousness-expanding benefits. He was eight when he first saw that his parents were not eternal: one morning he was floating around the house, all but levitating from room to room, and came into the kitchen to find a man reading the newspaper. It was his father, and only now did his son notice that he was going bald. "Enough, boy, stop your nonsense!" his mother cried, shaking him by the arms to bring him back. The doctor, whose stethoscope reminded him of two black snakes protruding from his satchel, assured them that it was quite normal: "Boys' stuff," and nothing that "a little solitude," as they called long spells of confinement, couldn't fix.

The good thing about being shut in a darkened room for hours is the introspection it fosters. You find out all about your ghosts; you may even learn to get along with them.

"We are the voices of the dead, voices like the buffeting of the sea," I said, doing my best disembodied-soul-beyond-the-grave impression for Fabiolo's answering machine.

"Come on, Mariachi," he said, eventually picking up. "That's Pavese, and you know it." Fabiolo certainly knew it—he knows everything.

A few days earlier, Fabiolo had told me about a

company he'd found in Tuscany that would come to your house to check for ghosts. The website had a photo of a sixteenth-century Medici villa with the caption: "Tests carried out by our team of parapsychologists, using the latest technology, have shown that the visions of former inhabitants were nothing more than chemical discharges caused by gas leaks from the kitchens." Millionaire North American expats would be my suspected target demographic for their services. But I have wondered whether young Schiavoni might not have been poisoned in some way. In the Rosario of his youth, homes were heated using gas from the streetlamps, which was known to contain high percentages of carbon monoxide, a common trigger for altered mental states and hallucinations.

Three years of life drawing with Costetti, and of Naná's high-octane spiritualism, turned out to be quite enough. The ghost of a ship's captain drowned in the Aegean popped up in one of the séances and addressed him: "*Torna alla nave, Schiavoni!*" He understood. A month later he was on his way home, moving into a crumbling mansion on the outskirts of Rosario. The property had black iron railings all the way around it, not that protection was necessary: the streets in this corner of Rosario, a neighborhood called Saladillo, became ice rinks in winter and corridors of dust and mosquitoes in summer, while the beetroots sold at the one local grocer were hard as stones. Almost all of the properties had a FOR RENT sign outside, since all the young people fled to the city more or less the second they turned sixteen. None of the few remaining were welcome in Schiavoni's home, where the lace curtains were permanently closed. He shut himself up too, like a seedpod, immersing himself in books about hypnotism, Mesmer, Abbé Faria. He once hypnotized himself in front of a mirror, and Musto, who had taken a house a couple of streets away, came in to find him frozen to the spot, almost completely stiff, his breathing so faint it didn't mist up on the silver plate Musto held to his mouth and nose. When Schiavoni came to, he declared that he had never felt so good in all his life: he had felt nothing. What a relief, to feel nothing!

And so there is the portrait he painted, the one containing a girl who I'm convinced is me: seated, gazing steadily out in her Sunday best, hat, pale lilac dress, coat two sizes too big. What she lacks in worldliness she makes up for in attitude; she can turn a look on you as withering as radioactive fallout, and her lips are sealed so tight that the sound of Velcro accompanies their parting. But inside she feels made of butter, and it takes all her patience, every ounce of her, not to lose her temper. Be a good girl! She wrestles nightly with the question: Is a person born bad, or does she become so? She sometimes gets angry; pushed for a description, she says it feels like a snake inching up her leg. The first time she felt it was in the square. Sitting playing with a friend on the grass, she suddenly took a rock the size of her fist and threw it straight at the other girl's face, leaving a small gash on her chin. She froze, watching the dark drops of blood fall onto her friend's white sneakers. She was like the boy from the story with whom none of the children want to play, knowing how he likes to secrete pebbles inside the snowballs. She still doesn't know what made her do it, but ever since then she has believed herself to be defective in some way, faulty by design. Some malignant gene come down to her on the maternal side. "Some little girls are born inherently good," wrote the great Laura de Nazianzi. "But not me."

One of the great moments in my life—one of those I-invented-the-wheel kind of moments—came in front of Schiavoni's *Girl Seated,* the kind of painting that leaves aside all pyrotechnics, all the razzle-dazzle of *ambitious* artists, and expresses something with the utmost simplicity. The critics branded Schiavoni a weirdo, a middling talent, a painter merely of instinct. But he was no naïf. It was in 1935, in the space of a few months, that people began to come around to him. An article in a Rosario newspaper censured the city for its failure to recognize him: one of the great Argentinian painters of all time was in their midst, and they had failed to notice. Schiavoni was in the insane asylum by this point. A couple of decades later Batlle Planas, the Argentinian Surrealist painter, called him "both sweet and cursed," and his detractors "imbeciles, swindlers, larvae: for you did not see his brilliance."

Another sad tale in the history of Argentinian painting. The story of my own encounters with painting, by contrast, is a happy one (though happiness interests only those who experience it; nobody can be moved by the happiness of others). To stumble upon the girl I once was, and to do so at this moment in my life, wasn't something I had been expecting: you only know what's gone once you've got it back. And though my new friend is a source of some considerable happiness, I try not to visit her too often.

"That's the way," says Fabiolo. "Get used to something, and you only become numb to it."

I am a woman hovering at the midpoint of life, but I still haven't lost my touch completely: it is within my power, for instance, to flit from the Schiavoni painting in the National Museum of Fine Arts to the Miguel Carlos

Victorica they hold in the Sívori Gallery. In other words, to make the shift from childhood to old age in an instant. In Victorica's *Aunt Cecilia*, we see a woman in her seventies, gray dress—the gray of photocopiers—and about her shoulders a fox-fur stole that looks stuck with thistles. She reminds me of Miss Brill, the middle-aged English teacher in the Katherine Mansfield story who lives in a small town on the French Riviera. Miss Brill goes for a walk every day in the Jardins Publiques, but the morning on which we join her is cooler than usual and she decides to take her fox-fur stole out of its box. At the park, she finds a bench and sits watching the couples strolling arm in arm: "They were odd, silent, nearly all old, and from the way they stared they looked as though they'd just come from dark little rooms or even—even cupboards!" Like Miss Brill, the Victorica produces an uneasy sensation in me, akin to trying to breathe underwater.

Go into any Argentinian art gallery and look around—but not too closely, keep your eyes unfocused to begin with. The first jolt you feel, like driving in a car and running over some unfortunate creature, is very likely to be a Victorica. And the jolt comes not from the subject matter but the way in which it is rendered. Nothing in Victorica is straightforward: scenes oddly framed, with inexplicable cut-off points; the heavy-handed application of the oils; the crusted impasto; the sheer amount of information crammed into the limited space of a canvas; and the way he somehow succeeds in plunging us straight into the *significance* of the scene in question. None of this has anything to do with his historical moment or, for that matter, his style; it is simply that the painter has found a way to express what it is like *to be him.*

Aunt Cecilia inhabits a limbo space like that of holographs. It is by no means a nice picture in any conventional sense, rather its allure lies in the fact it is an ugly picture, but of a tremendously attractive ugliness. Aunt Cecilia has been through a great deal, some of it extraordinary, but rather than change who she is, these experiences, like a sudden gust of wind stripping a tree of all its dead leaves, have given starker definition to an already present personality. She feels not nostalgia but something close to intrigue when she looks back over her life; for her it is a landscape to be contemplated dispassionately. It is a look I've seen before, on my daughter's face when she was wheeled around my parents' house once in her buggy, coming past bookshelves and pictures of animals on the walls. From one of the rooms, her grandfather emerged. He stopped in the doorway; gray Bermuda shorts, his skinny lower legs protruding from them, sagging like empty wineskins and mottled with dark, bruiselike patches. My daughter recoiled, in a sense cruelly, but not intentionally cruelly; not the gratuitous cruelty of young boys cutting off cats' whiskers or setting fire to toads. I saw it in her eyes: she was scrabbling to understand. She had just been presented with a picture of old age, though she had little idea what such a thing might be.

A few weeks ago I went on a scouting mission of old people's homes across Buenos Aires. I was looking on behalf of a close friend, who wanted to move her mother into one. After stopping off at what I can only describe as various circles of hell—more than homes, these were places to go and dump unwanted bags of bones—I came to one in which the walls were painted a calming celadon green. It was just a nice place. What I most liked was that it was so incredibly full of life; they put on all kinds of classes and sessions, though the yoga was really just a way to get the residents out of their armchairs. It felt like going back to schooldays, which might not sound inviting for everyone but, truly, it could be worse. Most of the residents seemed to go around in unbreakable pairs; they had best friends to eat lunch with and the best of enemies, too. The busy timetable gave their days shape; without routine they would have been as lost as a flock with no shepherd.

I felt relieved to get out of there: I'd found a suitable place and could end my searching, but once outside I also found that my legs were shaking a little. I put it down to the intensity of the place, the cumulative effect of all those old people, all those stories; nobody's immune to the occasional bout of butterflies. At home that night, I got into bed and called Fabiolo. I wanted to know what kind of old person he thought I was destined to become. The options, as I saw them, were: straight into la-la land, like the elderly lady who lives in my building and who takes her broom out for walks, convinced it's a poodle; going slowly, very slowly, so that one day someone looks in and all that's left is an indentation in the sofa; the way of hatefulness, becoming the kind of spiteful old crone that even cats give a wide berth; or the way of the genetically blessed, who reach their nineties in possession of all their faculties, the kind who are genuinely annoyed if they forget even a single word.

My father called to me from his room. My daughter didn't want to go inside, so I left her in the hallway and went in on my own. I asked how he was doing. "Just as you see," he said. "It shouldn't be called the Third Age, it's the Age of Halves: half deaf, half blind, half dead!" When I put my hand in his I found that his fingertips, once firm and full like a Chesterfield sofa, had had all the stuffing removed since last I touched them.

No one wants the bother of growing old, but I still find it interesting. It hasn't always been so: when I was fifteen I declared that I wanted to die young, with all the romance, all the literariness, that suggested. Dying, what bathos. Quite the cynic, I liked to think myself, going around saying that life was only worth the books you had written. My view has changed. Now I've had a look at the person I once was, I find myself interested in knowing what I'm going to become. My only hope is that when it comes time for the real giant leap, I'm in some kind of shape to make it.

Fabiolo goes out walking every day without leaving the comfort of his chair. He uses a computer program whose name I don't know, typing in, for example, "Vespignano," and instantly finding himself in the town of Giotto's birth. He strolls the streets, between dark olive trees and virtual cypresses, usually at dawn when everyone else is still asleep. "I do my best to avoid the good people of Vespignano, they can be a little intense first thing in the morning." He makes his way through the town and up along a sheer shepherd's path, going slowly. He's looking for something: the polished stone used by Giotto at the age of ten to show a certain Cimabue—passing through on his way to Florence—how to draw a sheep. The sheep that would be the starting point for all modern art.

"It's great, this walk," says Fabiolo, "it does me good. I'm feeling better all the time." Since I never actually lay eyes on him anymore, I take his word for it. He says his muscles are becoming toned again, and his washed-out cheeks have gone from paper white to pearly white. An easy change to put in words, but not so simple to bring about. I tell him I like the sound of it, and why don't we go together, him at his computer and me at mine, but he says I wouldn't be able to keep up; too easily distracted, too much of a scatterbrain. The program isn't perfect: if you try to hurry at all, if for example you want to see what lies two streets up ahead, it stalls, the picture judders, and the landscape breaks up into crazy waves and blocks until you get there. Fabiolo hates sudden changes: "So much. It's horrible, you feel like your body's turned to jelly." A leopard never changes its spots, which goes for sweet, spineless Fabiolo, too. I sometimes think he cooks up his supposedly public-facing self for my benefit alone—in an attempt to make *me* feel brave. "Anyway, I don't know why I bother trying to explain anything to you. I forget I'm talking to an *arrecha*." "*Arrecha*?" I say. "What's that?" "That's what they call intrepid women in Colombia," he says, though when I look it up later, the dictionary tells me an *arrecha* is a woman who is sexually aroused.

It's inevitable. You talk about yourself all the time, you talk so much that you end up hating yourself. When I get tired of me, of the constant mental gymnastics, it strikes me that ending up as a ghost wouldn't be the worst fate. I mean the kind of troubled spirit that's at the bottom of the phantasmal pile, the dumb blondes in the hierarchy of specters and poltergeists, tasked basically with frightening anyone unfortunate enough to live in an old building. "Rappers" is an old English word for these spirits. And I think that, if there were any vacancies, Fabiolo would be at the top of my list of people to spook. Go and shake his curtains on still nights, draw big question marks in toothpaste on his bathroom mirror, turn on the kitchen taps, and anytime he spoke to a girl on the phone (those dirty bitches, they should keep their hands off), mumble curses in my best Aramaic. I know, I'm terrible. To be a troubled spirit, to somehow disembody oneself—to dis-whatever my plodding brain, above all, and cast out my morose thoughts, the constant seething in my heart, to return to a state of mere energy, the random glimmering of the paranormal . . . To not think for a while, at least: that would be nice.

PITUCÓNES

Taciturn God, speak to us!

JULES RENARD

It was Anthony Powell, I think, who said we tend to get what we deserve in life. Domenikos Theotokópoulos was born in Crete in 1541—the man we call El Greco, or the Greek. This small island wasn't the ideal environment if a person had artistic inclinations, but here, growing up surrounded by both Venetian Catholics and Orthodox Greeks, he trained as a painter of Byzantine icons, an elongated, two-dimensional form of representation more concerned with invoking the divine than illustrating it. He moved to Venice, where he enriched his style with elements of Tintoretto, the most cinematic of the five immortals of Venetian painting. Next he made his way to Rome, where Michelangelo's work had the ascendency; the Italian would remain El Greco's benchmark for the rest of his life, and he stole more from him than he ever cared to admit. Having assimilated all the tricks he needed, he moved to Madrid, where, by way of a business card, and in an attempt to enter at court, he painted a portrait of Philip II. The king barely glanced at the painting; veering wildly at the time between the euphoria of victory at the Battle of Lepanto and depression following the death of his beloved Titian, he claimed it was a poor likeness and had it sent straight back. Did El Greco know by then that all observation takes place within? Was it only work he went in search of, or divine inspiration too, when he moved on to Toledo, a refined but also deeply religious city? It turned out to be a very good move; what the bluesman Robert Johnson described as "going down to the crossroads and coming back with terrifying new powers." Because in Toledo El Greco found his way as a peddler of pious images, starting out fairly conventionally but going on to produce staggering, seemingly sui generis work. Then one winter's night, an icy wind began to blow through his paintings. The space inside them grew constricted, and his figures, as if to adapt to these new climes, hollowed themselves out and lengthened upward. Anyone who saw these new paintings came away feeling giddy, suspecting the painter of having given them hashish and not tobacco to smoke after their supper of lamb stew. El Greco had simply given free rein to certain natural inclinations, allowing his theatricality and his appreciation of the natural world to combine with the lessons of his time in Italy. Having left when Mannerism was still in its pomp, he spent the rest of his days under the illusion that it remained the predominant style. It was a little like the World War II survivor who, having washed up on an island, was still hearing the bombs drop ten years after hostilities had ended.

Might fate in fact be more escapable than it seems? I asked myself this as the plane began its descent, my head brought out of the clouds by the winding roar of the landing gear directly beneath me. I was going to San Francisco to see my older brother for the first time in a decade. He moved there from Buenos Aires in 1990 because of the large number of rehab centers and drug programs on offer. We had never been close, for all that we were the two black sheep of the family: I always found him flaky, and it annoyed me that he'd never made use of his great talents; for his part, I know he always found me aloof. The thirteen-year age difference hadn't helped. The visit was his idea, after he heard about my work trips to Chicago. He had written to say I should stop by one time, say hello. In those days I was still managing, with a little assistance, to control my fear of flying, and so there I was that morning, about to touch down in San Francisco, scrubbing my face with one of the hot towels in an attempt to shake off the numbness into which the tranquilizer had cast me, as well as praying, in my altogether atheist way, for our natural sibling antipathies not to arise. In fact, there was nothing at all to worry about; an article in the in-flight magazine had steeled me, convincing me of something I'd long suspected: apparently, according to research carried out by a Hungarian physicist, our neurons are capable of self-reproducing, when the opposite has always been seen as the case. Cells called neuroglials have the capacity to generate new neurons, and these in turn can modify the phenotype, which in biological terms is a person's essence. "The mind is not immutable," said the writer, "neither its good points nor its defects." This being so, neither I nor my brother were the same people we had each previously known. There was a chance our new personalities might finally get along.

In the arrivals lounge a middle-aged man with a white

head of hair, white as the moon, held up a piece of paper with my name on it. "In case you didn't recognize me," he said, turning those big green eyes my way. Twenty minutes later, in the car, he made a comment that rankled me. Something sufficiently minor that I cannot now begin to remember it, but irritating enough to bring the pleasantries to a sudden stop. On arrival at his house I suggested a walk, so I could see a little of the neighborhood; a gray cloud had installed itself in my brain and was showing no signs of dissipating. When had it occurred to me that this trip might be a chance to heal old wounds? My brother must have been thinking along the same lines, because he too fell quiet. As we advanced, weaving now closer on the sidewalk, now farther apart, the steps of a gallery appeared in our path. I do not remember the outside of the building, only that there was a pennant by the entrance announcing an El Greco show. "Not a chance," he said. "Stay away from God at all times, that's my view. The farther, the better." His gaze grew distant, and I was reminded that he had been sent to Catholic school as a young boy.

I went in on my own, which was a relief, but as soon as I set foot inside I was reminded what a struggle El Greco is—a struggle with oneself. He's the kind of artist we fall for as teenagers, before we have taken the measure of painting as a whole, and while we're still at leisure to dive fully into our own private imaginarium. As we become more informed and, hence, cynical, we become less convinced. El Greco's unwavering dogmatism exasperates us, but so does his sensuality. We have difficulty accepting their coexistence in a single image; the mutual exclusivity of flesh and spirit has been drummed into us by now. This small San Francisco gallery had *View of Toledo*, a piece easily expressionistic enough to belong to the twentieth century. I recognized a reproduction *Christ in the Olive Grove* next to it; near the top, Jesus before the angel; underneath, a scattering of Apostles, sleeping on the floor like so many vagrants. A piece I have a weakness for. Not its theme—in fact I have little idea what the scene is supposed to signify—but rather the way in which everything in it seems suspended in the air. In it, gravity functions in reverse: something draws the figures skyward, sucking them in the direction of the clouds, like the bubbles in the lava lamps of my adolescence. The correct way to look at it, I thought, would be while doing a handstand; forget about the figuration and simply appreciate the scandalous sensuality of the brushstrokes strewing the oils this way and that across the canvas. Aldous Huxley must have been thinking similarly when he claimed that El Greco was such a visceral painter that, had he lived to see ninety, he would have ended up producing abstracts. Such were my thoughts as I looked up at the sky in the painting. A portentous sky, the kind beneath which only terrible or solemn events may occur, like a family member leaving home, or the erection of a cross.

Two months before my trip to San Francisco, the phone rang one morning during breakfast. It was very early, still dark out on the street, and the call made me jump—like fire alarm drills at school always used to. The man at the other end introduced himself as an artist, and both his voice and his name seemed vaguely familiar; he had a double-barreled surname that, still being half asleep, I didn't catch properly—only its sibilance. He was putting together a retrospective of his work, he said, and wanted me to write something for the catalogue. "Everyone's writing a piece," he said. "It's only you I'm missing." I have a policy in my work: never accept commissions (as Jules Renard said: "Writing for someone is like writing to someone: you're immediately forced to lie"). But he was insistent, saying it was vital that we meet, and something in his voice stopped me from refusing point-blank, although I knew full well I wouldn't end up taking the job. A few days later I went to see Santiago in his home studio, which was in an apartment in the Microcentro, a shanty-like part of town. A stooped man in a beige painter's smock came to the door. He had a pronounced underbite, giving him an obstinate look (Danilo Kiš would have said, "as though the lower part of his face were separated from the upper part by centuries of civilization"). He led me down a long, crumbling passageway lined with dusty-leaved banana plants. We came into an inner courtyard with a ceiling fashioned from semitranslucent tarpaulin, bathing the space in the kind of pearlescent light that usually accompanies rain. The bare kitchen had a number of paintings by other artists on the walls. In the rest of the rooms, which were even more spartan, the walls were covered with small religious images: Bible figures in jungle settings. I inspected these, before turning to consider my host. I had never before encountered a religious painter, or at least not a living one.

We sat down at the kitchen table. He had arranged some "dry biscuits"—aptly named—on a small glass plate, and there was a pair of chipped mugs, not matching. Santiago asked if I minded sharing a tea bag. It was now that I managed to place his way of speaking: it was plummy, upper class rather than provincial. Another black sheep, I thought, but kept the observation to myself; anytime I believe I recognize a fellow renegade, something in me instinctively draws back. I think it's about not wanting, in return, to be acknowledged as part of any group—yet more proof of my own snobbery, no doubt. But Santiago's mind was on other things. He chewed out his words, a little as though they were pearls, as though separating the real ones from the fake; he talked of God as though he knew precisely what he was referring to, and I couldn't bring myself to tell him that as a child, a precocious one, I had constantly given my poor parents the runaround on this very issue. I simply could never bring myself to feel excited by religion. For me the gods were amputees in marble, nothing more. Never having believed, I'd never been through any crisis of faith. To the point that, at the age of eighteen, I came up with my very own self-styled reverse renunciation: I announced my intention to enter a convent. But this mystical fervor had been so short-lived and now seemed so frivolous that I didn't feel like bringing it up. Santiago seemed then to notice that this wasn't my subject, and moved on: he had been wanting to tell me that he knew my older brother.

"Where from?"

"From the night."

He gave me a brown-toothed smile, his lower jaw sliding sideways as if independent of the rest of his body. But there was affection in the look—a desire to transmit more than it was able to.

Before he was old enough to go to school he was sent to Sunday school at the Santa Ana convent, under the watch of a wizened nun so tiny, he said, that her feet didn't touch the ground when she sat on a chair. Santiago was made to recite the Hail Mary, and if he stumbled, the woman could have been in a coma and she still would have marked him down. It was full marks for getting the words right, but if the delivery lacked conviction she'd only write it in pencil. This nun gave him a copy of *History of Religious Art*, with illustrations by Maurice Denis. Everything he had produced as a mature painter, Santiago said, was rooted in those images, though he had tried out other things initially. He made his first ever paintings in a barn in the country, shouldering aside saddles and harnesses to make space. His grandmother would stop in the doorway and make approving noises. Only she encouraged him in his calling; the rest of the family saw the endeavor as suspect, limp-wristed somehow. His art teacher in high school threatened to make him repeat the year because he didn't draw like the other pupils. When he did his military service, his double-barreled name made him a constant object of fun; the only time he was happy was on guard duty at night, a moment of solitude as the rest of the barracks slept. He fell ill one day and the military hospital to which he was sent ended up giving him a job, looking after NCOs who had come back broken men after fighting in Tucumán Province.

When his service was over, he spent weeks inside his

house. It wasn't until after the dictatorship ended that he resolved to set foot outside. All of his contemporaries looked askance at his work. Santiago fled his closed, upper-class circle and began moving in another just as inbred and just as all-consuming: the Buenos Aires art clique of the day. His entry strategy, the best way in, he thought, was to take a job in a gallery. This led to lots of time spent in bars and clubs, and he soon fell into the clutches of '80s nightlife, a monumentally dissolute time, a veritable Babylon—until AIDS came along. Most people will have an idea of how the story goes from there: whole weeks without any sleep, waking up to faces he didn't recognize, in places he didn't recognize, the bitter tang of the blowout burning his mouth. The panic attacks came back. He had not set foot in a church for over a decade but then, on one particularly desolate night, he got down on his knees and prayed: at first the words sounded empty as they came tumbling out, but gradually, little by little, his prayers began to have an effect. From that time on, every day at sunset he would put down his paintbrush and pick up his rosary beads; he had noticed that his mind started doing strange things when darkness fell: the fears, like fever, escalated at night. He went to Tupäsy María, a Benedictine monastery in a place called Corrientes. "The monks there taught me to see God in nature, and this God, which had aspects of the Guaraní divinities, became my closest friend." He began his *History of Religious Art* series: Bible stories transplanted to the jungles of colonial missionaries, all rendered in fine, nigh-vaporous brushstrokes. From time to time, he gave in to temptation: "At some point the light needs darkness, the one feeds off the other," he said, as we sat together in his kitchen. "At least that was what I told myself, if it meant I could carry on getting high."

After testing positive for HIV he moved back in with his parents: "My family welcomed me, but my sheets were sent out for cleaning every morning in case anyone caught anything." There was a portrait of James Lynch in the family living room, an ancestor who had been a mayor of Galway in the fifteenth century and had sentenced his own son to hang for murder. It is since then that killing someone without a legal trial has been known as "lynching."

"Every family has its own way of lynching. My family invented the genre, so you can imagine how long I lasted at home. And that was how I wound up living on a ranch, rented from the Church."

Just before this revelation, almost without realizing it, I had agreed to write something for the catalogue. He offered me a painting as payment. I said cash would probably be better. I was short of money as usual and I have never acquired the taste for collecting; deep down I think

I'm really a destroyer of images, and the few paintings I own languish in a pile in my utility room.

The piece I wrote was terrible, little more than a series of clichés. My problem was getting into the head of a man with such lust for life, who at the same time was moved by the death of Christ. It took me a long time to realize that this was down to my deficiencies as a writer, rather than his as a painter.

When I was studying history of art I obediently swallowed the line about El Greco having problems with his eyes. A severe astigmatism being the reason he saw the world as he did. I now know this to be a simplification, and one that fails completely to explain his cosmogony, just as Dostoyevsky cannot be boiled down to epilepsy or Keats to tuberculosis. What El Greco had was incredible vigor. When Jerónima de las Cuevas, the Spanish mother to his child, said she wanted to call the boy Michelangelo, the shouting that ensued left cracks in the palace windows. "Woman!" he is said to have cried, "do you not know how I hate that name!" There was no reason she would have; during his time in Spain El Greco had been careful to prevent the legend from spreading. But in art circles in Rome they still spoke of the day El Greco had visited the Sistine Chapel, and his having been so appalled by Michelangelo's bodies that he offered to repaint them. The view among the Romans was that he simply couldn't stand to be forever playing catch-up with his rival.

There's nothing more subterraneously oppressive than a family legend. My father was a talented sculptor, but became an architect; he used to say that in life we do what's required of us, not what we want. But I saw what this did to him over time, how his frustration grew. It wasn't helped by my mother, whose great aspirations for all of us were equal only to her deep-seated fear that we would fail her.

So it was with my brother. He excelled in anything he turned his hand to, was sporty, got top marks in just about every subject without even trying, and had a natural aptitude for photography. I remember seeing him going out with his camera, but I don't remember the photos themselves. He turned one of the bathrooms at home into a darkroom, leaving the photos to dry against the sky-blue mosaic tiles that covered one wall. I don't remember the exact moment his decline began, but I do recall Cyril Connolly's words: "Whom the gods wish to destroy, first they call promising."

A *pitucón*, according to the dictionary, is a young

person who is elegant, delicate, or promising. But *pitucón* is also an elbow patch, usually a leather one; that is, it prevents the rest of the fabric from tearing, while at the same time betraying its weakest point. My brother was a *pitucón*, the family scapegoat. His father left our mother after getting her pregnant; he had never wanted children but she let herself get pregnant anyway, thinking that might bring him around. She thought wrong. My brother never met his father, and when, later in life—after moving to the United States—he tracked down a phone number, and he rang him, it was only to be hung up on. He never saw him in the flesh. All he had was a negative our mother gave him; this struck me as a bad joke, macabre almost, although I don't believe she meant it as such: she was never so sophisticated in her cruelty. Her love for her son was always tortured, more a source of worry than happiness. She married my father when my brother was five. My father adopted him and he took our surname, but my brother never felt like one of the family. So he told me that afternoon in San Francisco. Although, the way I remember it, he was given all the privileges of the eldest and he eventually came to resemble my father more closely than any of the rest of us. When things went badly for him, he was sent away to the States; a part of me believes as a kind of banishment brought on by familial social embarrassment. But I also think it was his decision, that he wanted to go and look for his father, and that he stayed on there—for years—in hope that the phone might one day ring.

When I came out of the gallery my brother was sitting waiting for me on a bench. I had verbal diarrhea and he let me go on for about five minutes before suddenly cutting me off:

"What I can't stand about El Greco is the way he throws religion in your face." It was as though he had been thinking this the entire time I had been inside. After a pause, he added: "When I was a kid I prayed every single night not to become a priest."

I laughed at this; he did not. Then I remembered Santiago. I told my brother about meeting him a couple of months before. This seemed to make him uncomfortable. I said that Santiago had given me an autobiography to read, and he was planning on bringing it out to coincide with a retrospective of his work. Unaccountably curious, I read it in a single sitting, skipping the boring parts, until I realized in fact it was all boring parts, one leaden sentence after another. It felt like it had been written for his family's eyes only. Where was the juicy stuff, I wanted to know! This, to my surprise, made my brother furious:

"You really don't get it, do you? Stick to your paintings,

sis; when it comes to people, you don't have a fucking clue."

The day of my departure came. The flight was in the evening. My brother suggested we go to Muir Woods for the morning, a redwood forest half an hour from where he lived. There were three different trails you could take, and my brother suggested the longest one, which went through the woods and up toward the mountains. He said he knew the way but after an hour admitted he'd gone wrong. We took a shortcut; we got lost. Classic him. While we waited for a park ranger to appear and escort us back, my brother started cracking his knuckles. Only then did I notice how skinny his hands were. Like a figure in an El Greco, I said. "Not having a job," he laughed. "Pure upper-class indolence! They say it takes generations to cultivate; you need at least three hundred years to reverse it."

No park ranger showed and eventually we made our own way back. The forest lay silent. My brother moved from tree to tree like a dog following a scent, and I trailed behind him. Suddenly he called me over: an enormous redwood had been felled as a trail exhibit. It made my head spin to see the thousands of rings—and to think of the person sitting down to count them. Some of the rings had been highlighted and, on a small bronze plaque to one side, the year and a corresponding historical event laid out. It read:

A.D. 909: This tree is born.
1325: The Aztecs build Tenochtitlán.
1492: Discovery of the Americas.
1776: U.S. independence.
1990: This tree chopped down.

(The last one also being the year my brother left Buenos Aires.)

Santiago and I had agreed to meet at Florida Garden so that he could pay me for the article. He took a few handfuls of notes from the inside pockets of his raincoat; hyperinflation was rampant at the time. As he handed me the money, he glanced anxiously around, like this was a drug deal. I was slightly ashamed to even be charging for the article, surely the most insipid thing I'd come up with in years, but he seemed happy. We said cursory goodbyes, agreed we'd keep in touch. I headed home and immediately went to the corner shop across the street to buy things for the freezer. Vicente, the street's resident tramp, leaning against the abandoned Ford Torino in which he slept, shouted out to me: "Hey, girl, when are you going to clean up your housefront? It's looking pretty run-down."

Vicente was a man of many mysteries: he received visits every now and then from a young man with arms fully covered in tattoos, and the pair would spend the afternoon and evening conversing on the corner beneath the sheet-metal awning of a long-defunct grill house. The boy was a nephew of Vicente's and he wanted to convince his uncle to at least get a bed in one of the city's transition houses, but Vicente wouldn't hear of it. He seemed to like this way of life, he almost made an aesthetic statement of it, plus the fact that he had to be the most dandyish tramp in the world; I don't know where he went for his ablutions but he always looked immaculate, and at Christmas made a point of tying a red velvet ribbon around the trunk of the tree that stood between the Torino and my front door.

One day, the place next door was bought by a union boss with political connections. The builders worked day and night for a month to turn it into a luxury bachelor pad; people in the neighborhood said he'd had strobe lighting installed, along with a forty-foot shots bar and a heated pool in the living room. On Saturday nights Audis with tinted windows came and parked (double-parked) all the way along the street, and next morning the trash cans outside overflowed with empty champagne bottles.

Vicente's car was half on the sidewalk directly outside my front door and half in front of my new neighbor's, and one night this man came over to ask me to help convince Vicente to move to the other side of the street. I refused. Two days later, both Vicente and the car were gone.

He had lived on this street for fifteen years and had never caused any trouble. I don't know how he ended up here, or where he went afterward, but I remember a day when I saw him in the supermarket on the corner. I was queuing and he approached the checkout. The Chinese guy who ran the shop, without even looking up, flung a pack of cigarettes in his direction and sent him back out with a wave of the hand. Two elderly ladies behind me, very much *local* ladies—trolleys full of polenta, yerba maté, and ship's biscuits—watched but said nothing. Once Vicente had gone, I heard one say to the other: "And to think, all those young ladies who used to fall at his feet. Poor boy." Just like my mother, who anytime she talks about her sons adds that very same "poor boy" at the end.

Ten years after that day in the redwood forest, my brother was painting a wall in his apartment when his heart stopped beating. It fell to my two middle brothers to go to San Francisco for his belongings and the ashes, first because I had stopped flying and second because my mother didn't trust me: I had lost some inheritance documents pertaining to a property in Mar del Plata twenty years before, and was branded useless there and then. Once your family role has been assigned, that tends to be that.

I once heard that 90 percent of the dust inside a house is skin cells. This being so, my oldest brother was still there, really, when my other brothers walked in. I asked them to tell me what the house was like; people can lie, but their music collections, the posters on the walls, the furniture, no. They told me there was a can of paint on some newspaper on the floor, that the bed was unmade and had a light blue wool blanket on it with a rayon border, like the ones our mother used to place over us when we were little. They said there was a pizza box in the kitchen with two moldy pieces of pizza (this level of detail surprised me; I've never thought of my brothers as particularly observant), that the window in the bathroom had been blacked out and the lightbulb was painted red. Perhaps he'd taken up photography again, or perhaps he'd been having parties. The neighbor, a recovering alcoholic, said that after every relapse my brother decided to paint the whole apartment white. But the autopsy came back with no illicit substances.

When I think of him, I see him walking with his girlfriend in some woods in Uruguay, camera slung over his shoulder. I'm following them, I must be about eight.

Occasionally he turns around, annoyed that I'm there, and calls back at me to run along, to go home and work on my paper dolls. He looks at me with those green eyes—everyone else's in the family are dark. Then the image goes blurry, like swimming goggles misting up underwater, and frustrating though it is, there's nothing I can do; I can't will him into focus. The last thing I see before he slips away is a color, somewhere between green and brownish gray, like moss-covered rocks. But if I'm being completely accurate, a can of white paint, a blanket, two pieces of pizza, and a red lightbulb are the last of what I learned about my older brother; the last known thing of his wants and pleasures on this earth.

In a mysterious way, it is possible to predict one's fate; certain events present themselves to us in the form of premonitions. Not hypochondria, I don't mean that, but what Jean Rhys was referring to when she said: "And I saw I had known all my life that this was going to happen." For two years I'd had the sense that something was wrong inside me. When I was diagnosed with cancer of the thymus, it was almost a relief. The thymus is a part of the lymphatic system, a gland that is present from birth but that shrinks over time, eventually to be replaced by other cells. If this process fails to occur, sometimes the thymus can become a tumor. The Greeks thought the thymus was the soul, desire and life itself, possibly because of its position in the middle of the chest. So I had soul sickness. A nice thing to hear. I had lived my life until then like the quarry in a hunt, with the constant sensation that something was about to strike from some unknown quarter. They opened my chest, took out the tumor, closed me up, and sent me for radiotherapy. I now know that Montaigne was right when he said that "things often appear bigger in the distance than from close up." There is a kind of refinement process that goes on during illness, a paring away or casting off: as long, of course, as you manage to avoid self-pity, you actually find yourself worrying far less. I say this to a woman in the waiting room at the radiotherapy center, a professor of medieval literature with lung cancer who, because she is an inpatient, is ferried back and forth by ambulance for every session. She replies:

"I always wanted to have a *nice* illness."

We are a group of illuminati, here for our daily irradiation—and sometimes we do feel brilliant. There is one elderly gentleman with a very open face. His wife died sixteen years ago and he has never remarried.

"See he still wears the ring?" his sister says to me when he goes through for treatment. "I tell him it's time to start seeing other women, but he says love's a responsibility, and that he couldn't go around deceiving people."

He seems a good man, with the blandness that sometimes accompanies kindness, but I know by now there's no such thing as a simple heart. (Renard again: "This being good all the time is killing me.") To my right is the nurse with breast cancer and fleece trousers covered in cat hairs. She's angry because her public health insurance won't pay for the radiotherapy on her left breast; it would have been okay if the tumor had only been in the right one, but all the important organs beneath the left makes it a more expensive procedure. She specializes in keeping people's spirits up, dipping into a notebook of aphorisms that is always about her person. She picks one for me and reads it out: "Either you must decide to have the cancer, or the cancer will have you." I see what's happening with her: illness forces some people into bookishness. I never used to resort to quotations very much but in these past months I have read like a convict—yes, a convict, that's the word. I have also realized that being good with quotations means avoiding having to think for oneself.

The nurse comes back through from chemo with a patterned headscarf hiding the flyaway fuzz atop her perfectly round head. "Not a single hair may fall from our heads without God's permission," she tells me. She was a nun before becoming a nurse, and after that a single mother, in a village in Patagonia the name of which I forget, along with any details except that it is a very windy place (my mother says my memory has deteriorated since the general anesthetic, and it is true, I used to remember everything).

"I said to the doctor the other day," whispers the woman on her left, her face puffy from steroids, "either you help me live, or you do something to help me die. One or the other."

Across from us sits a thoracic surgeon who is also here for radiotherapy. His face is gaunt and he is wearing an elegant overcoat that looks far too big on him now. When I show him my scar, his eyes light up. He admits that he misses rummaging around in people's chests, that for him there was always something of a treasure hunt about it. He also says—half to himself, because he still isn't used to the shoe being on this foot, to seeing things from this side of the doctor's desk—that death is just as unreliable as life.

The only one who doesn't join in the conversation is the Buddha: a man of about forty who always sits in the corner next to the money plant, eyes shut, hat in hands. He has some kind of cancer of the head; a telltale roseate scar encircles his left ear. I've become a dab hand now when it comes to identifying illnesses. I've seen him open his eyes and get up and walk with no trouble. I've heard his irascibility when arguing with the receptionist over the waiting times, and over canceled sessions when the machine has broken down, but he's never said a word to any of us. Sometimes the last thing the ill want is the company of their own kind. In this waiting room, with its yellow walls, its orange armchairs, and a plasma screen constantly playing the Cooking Channel with the volume down low, where morning after morning we wait for our names to be called, he is the Prince of Aquitaine: sporting his cursed lute, and a black melancholic sun always at his shoulder. After Mrs. Aguirre Velazco, it's my turn, and she's after him. I remember the surname Aguirre Velazco because my house is in Villa Crespo and in Villa Crespo it goes Calle Loyola, Calle Aguirre, then Calle Velazco.

"Cold front. Snow expected," it said on my car radio this morning. I saw them from the corner, men and women in dark coats lining up at the Radiotherapy Center doors. They come here hoping for extra time. Above, the sky is gray, the mortal gray of an ice rink, and when the first flakes start to fall they all look up, but not in surprise; these are not the kind of people to surprise easily.

Renard again: "How monotonous snow would be if God had not created crows." The snow drifts slowly down, swirling, forming thin lips at the edges of roofs, covering the pavements in a sheer, lacelike layer, and I lean over to the glove compartment and take out the black woolly hat I put there when all of this began. This is the first time I put it on, pulling it down over my ears, getting out of the car and walking straight toward them. A quiet joy comes over me as my feet touch the ground, poetic joy, I think they call it. I'd give my right arm to remember who called it that.